Punto de cruz

JAZMINA BARRERA

Translated from Spanish by
CHRISTINA MACSWEENEY

CROSS STITCH

TWO LINES
PRESS

Two Lines Press
582 Market Street, Suite 700, San Francisco, CA 94104
www.twolinespress.com

ISBN: 978-1-949641-65-3
Ebook ISBN: 978-1-949641-54-7

Design by Sloane | Samuel
Needle illustration by Em Randall
Printed in the United States of America

Library of Congress Cataloging-in-Publication Data:

Names: Barrera Velázquez, Jazmina, 1988- author. | MacSweeney, Christina, translator.
Title: Cross-Stitch / Jazmina Barrera ; translated from Spanish by Christina MacSweeney.
Other titles: Punto de cruz. English
Description: San Francisco, CA : Two Lines Press, [2023]
Summary: "The story of three childhood friends-Mila, Citali, and Dalia-over the course of their friendship and into adulthood, fused with the cultural history of sewing"
Identifiers: LCCN 2023010761 (print) | LCCN 2023010762 (ebook) | ISBN 9781949641530 (hardcover) | ISBN 9781949641547 (ebook)
Subjects: LCSH: Women--Fiction. | Embroidery--Fiction. | Cross-stitch--Fiction. | LCGFT: Novels.
Classification: LCC PQ7298.412.A786 P8613 2023 (print) | LCC PQ7298.412.A786 (ebook) | DDC 863/.7--dc23/eng/20230313
LC record available at https://lccn.loc.gov/2023010761
LC ebook record available at https://lccn.loc.gov/2023010762

1 3 5 7 9 10 8 6 4 2

This book is supported in part by an award from the National Endowment for the Arts.

To those women who have
embroidered with me.

Don't be sad, Lilí. You'll find the thread,
and you'll find the spider.

— Elena Garro, *Un hogar sólido*

It was around noon when I got into the shower. The damp patch on the bathroom ceiling was spreading, making the paint peel and feeding a colony of fungi, initially green and then red, like a moldy tortilla. During the first year and a half of my daughter's life, I used to let things like that just happen, too weary and overworked to worry about them, but now they're beginning to irritate me.

I walked naked into the bedroom, chose some clothes, but before I had time to dress, I heard my cell phone vibrating. The screen showed a Facebook message from Valentina Flores. It took me a moment to remember that she was Citlali's aunt: I'm devastated, Mila dear, my heart breaks every time I write this. Citlali had an accident, she drowned in the sea in Senegal. We're bringing her ashes back. I'm so sorry, Mila. She adored you and I know you adored her.

My head hurt like I'd been punched in the face.

Like someone was trying to suck my brains out through my eyes. I don't know how long I sat there on the bed, hugging my towel, trying to cry silently so my daughter and Andrés wouldn't hear. Brief, painful images flashed across my mind, one after another like bats in a cave: Citlali's face, her lips blue; her arms battling against the current; her open mouth swallowing salt water; her body floating amid strands of seaweed, spume, and plastic bottles. All this mingled with the laughter and shrill voice of my daughter: she was singing and dancing with her father to an album by The Breeders. My damp hair was dripping down my neck. It was hard to breathe.

After a while, Andrés left her playing with a toy and came into the bedroom. Which friend? he asked. You don't really know her, I replied. You only met her once. Is she the one with the parvovirus dog? No. The punk? The engineer? The child-hating redhead, the blonde child-hater?

I smiled and, as I did, realized that my nose was bleeding. Andrés went to fetch cotton balls to stem the flow. I didn't have the strength to explain who Citlali was. I didn't even try, not until later, until that night.

Is she the one who lives in Spain?

No, that's Dalia. Citlali was always moving around. She finally settled in Brazil but had to travel a lot because she worked for that environmental NGO.

Right, and I met her? Was she the woman with black hair and dark complexion?

No, that's Dalia too. Citlali had short, fair hair and was really skinny.

She wore kind of masculine clothes, right?

Yes, that's her.

And you three were childhood friends?

Well, we met in middle school.

But then you were at college with Dalia.

Same department, different majors.

Ah, I think I know who she is now.

I woke very late the next morning, and the first thing I did was text Dalia. Her reply came back after a few hours. It simply said, Yes, I know. I had no idea what else to say, and I guess she didn't either.

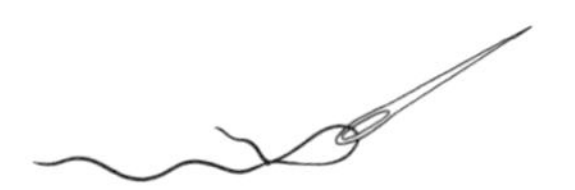

The Spanish verb *bordar* is derived from the Indo-European *bhar,* meaning point, bristle, hole. This, in turn, has an etymological association with the Latin *fastus*, from which we get *fastuoso* and *fastidio* (lavish and annoyance). In both Spanish and English, the verb has a common root in the Old French *brouder*, meaning "the side of a boat" (as in starboard). And this is how it relates to embroidery, which was used to decorate the edges of fabrics.

The tenth-century Anglo-Saxon *Exeter Book* contains an ambiguous extract: *Faemne aet hyre bordan gerised*. The ambiguity lies in that *bordan* can mean table, embroidery, or, as above, edge. One possible translation is, "A woman's place is at her embroidery." A looser translation might be, "A woman's place is on the edge of the abyss."

I passed days in a state of profound sadness about Citlali's death, trying to distract myself with the routine tasks of caring for my daughter—something that required my full attention—living in the absolute present, but, even so, in each quiet moment I returned to a mix of sorrow and anger. And that's still the case: I'm furious with her for having let herself be defeated, for never managing to defy her stupid father or recover from her mother's death, for never managing to get over herself. At my deepest levels of egoism, I also reproach her for having given up on this world my daughter now shares, for having abandoned me in my new life, just when I most need her humor and affection. But another part of me is angry with myself. I feel powerless and at the same time responsible for not having taken better care of her. Waves of fury and misery wash over me.

It took me two days to reply to Valentina's message. I told her how deeply her news had affected me and that I was anxious to hear more details of what had happened. She repeated pretty much what she'd said in her previous message: Citlali had drowned in the sea in Senegal; she went in for a swim and never came back. They found her body on the beach hours later. None of that clarified whether it had been suicide or an accident.

Her father had the ashes. He'd put them in the living room of his apartment. I wanted to know exactly where but decided it would be best to see for myself.

I asked if they were thinking of holding some kind of leave-taking ceremony. Yes, she replied, I know we should, but I'm not up to it. I'm in pieces. Would you help us? I didn't reply immediately, but then said of course I would. I asked her to suggest a date, said I'd contact Citlali's friends and think about what kind of event it should be.

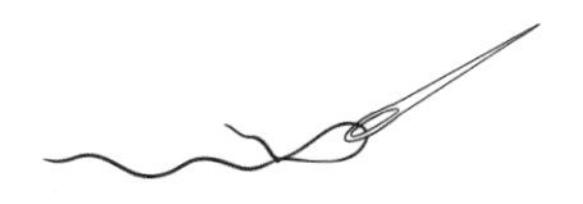

I decide to set my embroidery aside for a while to make the calls. For days, I've been feeling guilty about putting things off. I haven't worked out how to sew and think about Citlali without pricking my fingers. I've set myself the task of calling people today, but it's the hardest thing ever. Somewhere, I have an old address book that must contain the cell phone numbers of high school friends. A few may still work.

I rummage through the messiest drawer in my desk, but before I can find the addresses I come across the journal I kept during our trip to Europe and sit down to leaf through it. Since Citlali's death, the memories we shared have been weighing on me because she's no longer here to help me carry them all. Images, scenes, and conversations that I didn't realize I'd forgotten emerge from all sides, secrets and memories that belonged exclusively to Citlali and me, and others that we shared with Dalia. In this journal there are traces of those three-person memories: photos, entries about the places we visited together, and a sizeable collection of odds and ends glued in—museum, gallery, and subway tickets; pressed leaves; and even a gum wrapper. There's enough information here, in the scattered phrases and on those scraps of paper, to reconstruct and so recall the itinerary, although I know perfectly well that my memories aren't accurate, that I make half of them up. More than half. That doesn't bother me.

I find an Air France ticket and recall that journey when we were nineteen, as if I were remembering a dream. In the final year of high school Dalia started working in a bookstore in Coyoacán on the weekends, but her airfare had been a present from her lesbian aunt. Both Dalia's parents and mine were separated—something that was already pretty common by then—but we were also united by a coincidence that seemed to us more unique: We both had single lesbian aunts (we used to fantasize about setting them up on a blind date, but they never agreed) who were like second mothers to us, but with a little more spending power and much more capitalist views on life than our biological ones. My aunt bought my ticket without complaint, although I'm sure she had to pay for it in a number of installments. At the very last minute, my father, who was four years behind with the alimony, turned up with an unexpected—and no doubt guilt-inspired—wad of dollars that I stashed in my bra, as my mother advised.

The reason for the trip was to see Citlali, who'd already been living in France for six months. A few days before we set off, she sent us an email saying that she was flat broke and hadn't eaten for two days. At that point the trip became urgent: We were going to rescue our friend, save her, and—as far as I was concerned—bring her back home with us, although that last part was a bone of contention between Dalia and me.

On the morning of our departure, Citlali sent another email, as terse as a telegram, simply stating that she couldn't come to London but would catch up with us in Paris the following week. We replied, asking what had happened, if everything was all right, begging her to reconsider, saying we'd lend her enough money to get by in London. But deep down we knew there was nothing to be done; Dalia and I would see London on our own, and then if Citlali didn't come to Paris, we'd go to the town in Provence where she was staying and find her there.

Although an out-and-out atheist, my mother made the sign of the cross over me when she said goodbye. But at least she'd agreed to stay home. Dalia's, on the other hand, insisted on taking us to the airport. She checked we'd charged our phones, had the address of Dalia's cousin in London and Citlali's phone number in case of an emergency. I already told you she's not coming to London; we're going to meet up in Paris, replied Dalia impatiently. Just in case of an emergency, repeated her mother. What kind of emergency is she going to deal with from France? Dalia snapped and I intervened, taking a strand of Dalia's hair between my fingers and saying, Your red streak is definitely pink now. I know, it faded in no time, but I think I like it better this way. She smiled, forgetting about Marie—her mother—for a moment. Marie heaved a sigh, muttered a "these things are sent to try us"—she hated Dalia dying her hair—gave her daughter a big farewell kiss on each cheek, and asked me (rather than her daughter) to let her know when we arrived in London.

Dalia and I joined the interminable check-in line. We were dressed for winter, though the weather in Mexico could hardly be called cold. I was jealous of Dalia's coat, which was lovely: black and fitted at the waist. Mine looked like a garbage bag. My mother had insisted on buying me one with goose-down filling. No polyester or those plastics that were destroying the planet. I knew better than to argue about things like that, but the only suitable coat we could find was a couple of sizes too large and had a weird florescent yellow design on the hood. There had been a time before that trip when Dalia's pet name for me had been Toucan, though we'd forgotten why. When I put on my coat, she pulled up the hood and called me by that name again. We laughed, and she hugged me.

Or tried to hug me, while stooping to support her giant suitcase—the drag handle had broken the moment we arrived at the airport. She also had a carry-on bag, a purse, and a small backpack. I asked why she was bringing so much stuff, and she said it was winter clothes. And in that bag? Food for the plane; everyone says the in-flight meals are disgusting. And in that other one? My embroidery things. I need something to pass the time, she said, because I can never sleep in uncomfortable places. Will they let you through with your needles? I asked. I've only got one, and it's inside my needle case; I don't think they'll notice.

My embroidery was at the bottom of my check-in bag. I was doing a black tree with black birds on black fabric. Dalia hadn't seen it yet. For the flight, I'd also brought books, an MP3 player loaded with a playlist, and headphones with splitter cables so we could listen at the same time. Dalia used to say she knew nothing about music but liked what I listened to, so she was learning that way.

On the plane, we were in a row with three seats and were almost certain we'd have them to ourselves, with elbowroom and space to stow our carry-on bags. It felt good to be traveling alone; we'd just finished our first semester at college and were in a fascinating period of our lives, brimming with possibilities. For the first time, we were studying things we'd chosen to study, taking our initial steps along a road that was completely our own. There's a song by Françoise Hardy that says we're rulers of the world when we're twenty, and despite being still only nineteen, we felt we had that world at our feet, were flying over it, exactly as we'd be doing very shortly.

Just as the doors were about to close, a young, almost handsome priest boarded the plane, and we had to squeeze together to let him get to the window seat of our row. He gave us a friendly greeting, read the safety instructions a couple of times, then opened a book called *Tears of Hope* with a picture of a frog on the front cover. Dalia took out her embroidery. She was halfway through a bookmark with a really intricate design of red flowers in cross-stitch: a birthday present for her aunt—gifts were our favorite pretext for embroidering. I was reading Shirley Jackson's *We Have Always Lived in the Castle*, which had me hooked: The main character was just like me—or partly like me; I was much less brave but more cheerful—and while reading, I was high on the idea that we were at the very least sisters under the skin, that I understood her dark side because it was also mine.

The priest laid aside his frog book and said he didn't want to bother us, but would it be okay if he asked a question. I nodded. He said he couldn't pass up the opportunity because he had very little contact with girls our age and was curious to know if we believed in God. My view was that there was no way of knowing if God existed, but I thought we had to live as if he, she, or it didn't. I'm certain there isn't one, said Dalia; all religions, Christianity in particular, are interesting but dangerous fictions. Ah, I see, responded the priest, and embarked on a convoluted argument with Dalia about the proofs for and against the existence of God. I very quickly tuned them out but could no longer concentrate on Jackson, so I put my headphones on and started watching a Hugh Grant movie. Dalia, Citlali, and I had discussed the Hugh Grant enigma once or twice, unable to decide whether he really was good looking—whether he seemed handsome because he was likeable, or if it was just that so much talk about him being handsome had made us believe it, even though he actually wasn't. I wanted to ask Dalia if that was what we mean when we say someone is attractive but didn't because I could tell that the argument with the priest was in full flow, and she was beginning to lose her temper and raise her voice. I heard her quoting from the apocrypha and German philosophers I'd never read. What do you two girls know? You're just a couple of rich kids whose parents are sending them to Europe, the priest almost screamed. And you're just an old sleazebag who can't get it up, and probably a pedophile to boot, replied Dalia with a conclusive gesture, and then she stood up to go to the toilet. When she returned, she immediately took out her copy of Natalia Ginzburg's *The Little Virtues* and buried her head in it to the exclusion of all else. After a while, the priest also got to his feet. He asked permission to get past us and, as a peace offering, returned down the aisle with two of the chocolate popsicles they were handing out at the rear of the cabin. We accepted them guiltily. They looked delicious. He tried to apologize and continue his conversation with Dalia, but she told him firmly that she didn't want to talk. She stopped licking the popsicle, finished it off in bites, and, frowning, read for an hour more. Then she slept, balled up like a black bean with the hood of her coat up. When Hugh Grant finally found happiness, I donned a mask, put in earplugs, and slept too.

As we were disembarking, I realized that my Shakespeare professor had been on the same flight. Goodness knows why we hadn't seen him when we were boarding. It was a coincidence, but not a huge one considering that it was the last weeks of the college vacation. I liked his classes, even if his overdone irony and melancholy man-of-letters persona drove me slightly crazy. I thought he liked me because I was one of the few students to actively participate in the class.

We greeted one another and walked to the baggage area together. Eduardo was visiting a former student who was now living in London and dating Iris—a friend who had the same major as me. As she was also staying in the city during the vacation, Dalia and I had planned to meet up with her a few days later. Eduardo knew London well and told us about the bookstores, pubs, and his favorite museums and galleries. He was particularly looking forward to visiting a German neo-expressionist exhibition at the White Cube and jotted down the name of the artist (Anselm Kiefer) on the back of his card in case we were interested. Dalia's luggage arrived quickly, Eduardo soon had his, and there was only mine to come. It turned out that it had gone missing somewhere. I was told it would be located and sent to my lodgings as soon as possible. I took one of Dalia's bags, and the three of us walked to the underground station. Eduardo helped us to buy tickets for the correct zones, and we traveled on the same train for part of the journey. I experienced a strange thrill every time I heard the man announce, Mind the gap between the train and the platform.

Eduardo complained about the cold—he didn't have a warm overcoat and joked that they weren't available in hobbit-size. I laughed; Dalia didn't even giggle and suggested in all seriousness that he go to the teen's department. The male voice announced that the next station, where Dalia and I had to change trains, was closed. In a panic, we made a spur-of-the-moment decision, said goodbye to Eduardo, and scrambled off before the doors could close. Our large, foldable map showed a bus route that would take us directly from there to the apartment.

The elevator was out of order, so we had to lug our suitcases up dozens of steps to street level. We exited close to a square and, silhouetted against the night sky, saw a large gray building topped by a dome. I think that must be something, I told Dalia excitedly—we later learned it was the National Gallery. The red double-decker buses seemed unreal; we pointed them out to each other and then realized there was a stop nearby, but however hard we tried, it seemed impossible to work out which direction to take. In the end, we chose the first bus that came along.

Dalia tried to push her gigantic suitcase into the small space reserved for strollers. A woman with a young child kindly moved hers to make room. I sat down next to the window and watched the passing streetlights and cars. Dalia, staring at the woman with the stroller, asked me—out of the blue—if I knew where you could get an abortion in Mexico City. I was startled because I assumed it was for herself, but she quickly clarified that it was for someone at school—I knew all her friends, but she wouldn't mention a name. It had to be somewhere cheap because the father wasn't involved, and her friend didn't want to tell her mother. Is the mother a strict Catholic? I asked. No, a strict

Buddhist, she answered. I'm not sure what kind of Buddhism, but it prohibits killing even a fly and there's no way to convince her that abortion isn't killing. I said I couldn't think of anywhere but knew that a cousin of mine had had an abortion a while back. I'd ask her. We should have studied medicine, said Dalia; it's the only subject worth taking these days. Maybe, but there are so many needles and knives, and those poor students never have time to sleep. I love sleeping; I need to sleep, I told her. It's not such a big deal for me, responded Dalia. We fell silent, looking out into the night, so different from ours.

And, of course, we were going in the wrong direction. At the next stop, we got off and attempted to correct our mistake but got it wrong once more: We were used to consulting the *Guia Roji* of the interminable Mexico City and had never imagined that map reading could be so complicated. When we finally boarded the right bus, we wearily flopped into our seats, laughing. It was just before eleven at night. This time, we managed to get off at the correct stop, supposedly near the building where we were to stay. We walked along in silence, thinking that the modern gray architecture was rather bland, but gradually understanding that the neighborhood did have a certain charm. A jogger wearing shorts and a sleeveless shirt passed on the opposite sidewalk, and I commented that either he must be crazy or it was perfectly normal in England for people to go running at all hours in such low temperatures. Normal—it helps the body warm up, said Dalia, who jogged occasionally and used to go to a gym that Citlali and I had also joined for a few months. Only Dalia made any use of the membership; Citlali and I passed the time commenting on people's clothing and imagining their lives. We were seriously worried about a man who, despite coming every day, still seemed to be gaining weight, and there was a diminutive fitness instructor who used to make us laugh when he called both the male and female bodybuilders *dolls*. None of them seemed to mind.

Something wasn't right: We'd crossed the junction where the street we wanted should have been, but there was no sign of it. In desperation, we stopped at a taxi stand and asked a driver to take us to the address we'd written down. That's just around the corner, luv, he said with a laugh. It'll cost you. Sure you want to pay? We were sure.

We'd mistaken the name of the building for a street, hence our confusion. In Mexico, buildings don't have names, we told the driver, who responded with another laugh, telling us exactly how much we owed him. We extracted a few bills from the wads secreted in our bras, paid, and got out.

In Oaxaca State, the Chinantec, Mixtec, Chatino, and Triqui peoples all share variations on a myth that derives partly from the *Popol Vuh* of the K'iche' Maya of Guatemala and partly from the *Leyenda de los soles*, the legend of the suns. The myth refers to a weaver (the Chinantec call her the Señora Tepezcuintle), the wife of a deer, who adopts or conceives twins. In some versions she gets pregnant while she's at work and during her pregnancy weaves the various layers of the sky on her loom. The twins born to her become Sun and Moon, and they have many adventures. They kill a monster with shining eyes by strangling it with a length of yarn or a woven sash. Then they throw a ball of thread into the sky, inaugurating time, and climb up the thread. They also rape a woman, who curses them and throws weaving sticks at them—the face of the moon is scarred by the sticks. The furious woman then casts the bloodied fabric she was weaving to the ground, and ever since women have had to menstruate.

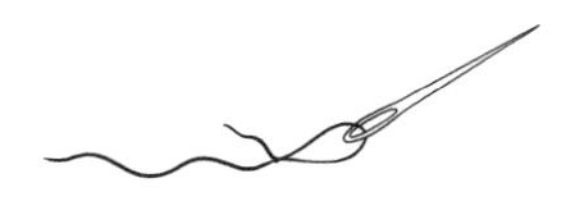

Echinoderms—starfish—can regenerate lost arms, an ability not shared by mammals. To some extent, but by no means totally, we have compensated for this lack with needles and thread.

My grandmother always used a thimble. She was taught to embroider by her aunt in the small Yucatán town where she grew up but didn't discover thimbles until she moved to Mérida. She thought they were marvelous and used to say that sewing machines, washing machines, and thimbles had changed her life. I never found thimbles comfortable to wear, but there was a period when I spent so much time embroidering that I got calluses on my fingertips, and if I pricked myself, the needle would never go deep enough to draw blood. Citlali would give a nervous giggle when I'd ask her to prick me to demonstrate the quality of my calluses. Remembering her laughter makes me want to laugh too, but I stop myself so as not to wake my daughter, who's sleeping in the next room while I embroider her name on the backpack she needs for her first day at nursery school. Laughter has to be one of the hardest things in the world to hold back, almost harder than tears. Citlali and I had a friend—not a particularly close one—we called Pi, who invited us to her house one day and kept us there for quite a while to watch her practicing her laugh. As she didn't like her own, she was attempting to find a new one and tried out several options on us. She took the whole thing very seriously, and Citlali and I had to make an enormous effort not to succumb to wild, injudicious bursts of laughter.

Citlali had a raucous laugh: cackles like thunderclaps exploding from her wide mouth, often followed by an attack of hiccups—I once witnessed her father scolding her, saying there must be something wrong with her to laugh like that, and that's why she got hiccups. She was always laughing, and our teachers disliked her for it. She used to pass jokes, notes, and drawings to the girls nearby with the skill of a Russian spy. Laughter sparked around her like Bengal lights; teachers had the feeling that it was aimed at them, and they were often right. She'd laugh at anything and anyone, herself most of all. But she got good grades, did well on tests, and there was no real evidence of disobedience, so every week, when she was sent to the principal's office with a yellow or red slip, no one could put their finger on exactly what she'd done, and it was, therefore, almost impossible to punish her. She progressed from year to year under a constant cloud of suspicion.

During the first months of middle school, Citlali and I sat at opposite ends of the room. At recess, she'd chat with a group of girls on a bench by the first-floor balcony, their eyes fixed on the soccer field as if they were doing a radio commentary on the game. From time to time, Dalia would join them—she and Citlali had been in elementary school together—but her main friends were the sporty types, the good-looking girls who were no longer little kids, who played soccer or volleyball in the afternoons, had boyfriends, wore low-cut tops, and could dance.

I was envious and slightly afraid of those girls, all except Dalia. Or maybe I felt that way about her too, but I also admired her and would sometimes smile at her when we passed—she always smiled back. Dalia was the smartest student in the class. Perhaps not in math or biology, but she was the pet of the wise, warm-hearted teacher with a beard who taught Spanish language and literature and used to recommend books to us that I hated—*The Unbearable Lightness of Being* or *Siddhartha*—but that he succeeded in convincing me were good, or at least fun to talk about. He was my favorite teacher, and Dalia was his favorite student. Her spelling was perfect, she could read aloud more fluidly than anyone else, without ever making mistakes, she mapped sentences on the board in the blink of an eye, and had very clearly gotten through more books than the rest of us put together. That combination of beautiful, elite student and sports star brought her admirers and detractors in equal measure. Every so often, a piece of graffiti would appear in the girls' bathroom saying, "I ♥ Dalia," followed by another: "Dalia is a slut."

On the first day of class in that new school, during recess, I lolled on the balcony next to a very pretty blonde girl with a shrill voice who exchanged a few words with me and, at some point, commented on the bouncy boobs of one of the basketball players on the court. Apparently, her boobs bounced because she wasn't wearing a bra. Apparently, that was a mistake. I didn't wear a bra either. I thought my breasts were too small to require support, and anyway, my mother detested bras, unless the idea was to burn them on a feminist pyre. As soon as I heard the girl's comment, I felt dumb and was instantly conscious of the way my own boobs, however small, wobbled under my blouse; despite the heat, I kept my sweater on for the rest of the morning, and that afternoon—having won an argument I'd been convinced I'd lose—my mother took me shopping for underwear. After that incident, it became clear to me that I was one of the misfits, and as a result, I started to hang out with others of the same ilk.

The misfits were: Manuela (I think that was her name), a flautist with a permanent smile who wore orthodontic headgear and was good at the hard sciences; Sol, another short, thin, hyper-shy girl who, despite her name, radiated an almost total lack of charisma but made up for it with huge amounts of kindness and warmth; Lourdes, who had giraffe eyes and, instead of taking notes in class, spent the whole time combing her long red hair—she had an excellent memory so didn't need notes; and then there was me. I wouldn't have known how to describe myself at that time and, as you might expect, still don't.

One of the things that made me a misfit was that I didn't even enjoy hanging out with the others much. I hardly ever left the classroom. At lunchtime, I'd stay there reading, sketching, eating plums and peanut candy. I used to draw and write to keep a hold on my imagination, certain that I was going to lose it, since all adults lost their imagination at some point. I clung desperately to the childlike gaze that finds motives for curiosity and astonishment in everything it encounters. The people I talked to most were the teachers, who liked me because I was hardworking. In my alternative elementary school, we had never been given homework, so that task was a complete novelty I even looked forward to. I might not have been the smartest person in the class, but I was probably the nerdiest.

But, nerd that I was, my level of English was too low to get me into the advanced group for that subject. In my elementary school, English had been considered the language of imperialism, and we'd only been taught the basics. Nevertheless, that was enough to earn me a place in the smaller, second group with Citlali. None of our own regular friends were there, and our desks were next to each other. The first time we spoke was when Citlali pointed to the teacher's backpack: the front zipper was open, and a pack of strawberry-flavored condoms was poking out. I think Tania—our biology teacher—must like strawberries, Citlali said, and we both laughed while the teacher went on writing up exercises on the board. The condoms finally fell out of the backpack, and Citlali got hiccups from laughing so hard. We spent the whole lunch break together, trying every cure we knew: holding your breath, drinking water from the wrong side of the glass, a sudden shock. But that had us laughing even harder and made her hiccups worse. They went away on their own later, as we chatted.

We began teaming up in that class for partner work, which usually consisted of writing out the lyrics to Beatles' songs or completing question sheets about Tim Burton movies. From The Beatles (whom Citlali detested, as she'd had to spend her Sundays listening ad nauseam to cover versions by her father's band, Los Cara Abajo) we moved on to talking about music in general; we both liked Aterciopelados and Blondie. Moreover, we watched the same programs on MTV and loved Lucky Charms cereal. Our senses of humor were similar; with Citlali, I discovered the delights of making fun of people behind their backs. We had recurrent in-jokes, the targets of which were, for instance: a boy we nicknamed "Naked" because one day he came to school in a T-shirt longer than his shorts, so it looked as if he were in the buff from the waist down; our biology teacher, Tania, who used to call for silence by emitting a very realistic neigh at full volume; and a classmate who only ever talked about soccer and was incapable of understanding any concept that couldn't be explained to him with the aid of a ball. But most of the time we laughed about the things we did ourselves: Citlali's perfect imitation of Edith Piaf or the presentation about Neanderthals we shot on her father's camcorder for a world history class, in which my nipple appeared for a moment because I hadn't tied my tiger-pattern throw properly.

I began spending some lunch breaks with Citlali, and then all of them, and we'd meet up after class to pass the afternoons together too. I deserted the giraffe and all the other misfits and joined Citlali's group, although my relationships with Pi—the girl with the studied laugh—and the others were fairly superficial: Citlali was my real friend.

It was on a day when Citlali and I spent the recess together in the classroom that Dalia spoke to me for the first time. She said, I like your nose. One of our classmates was making a gossip book, where we had to write down the name of the person we thought was the best looking, who had the loveliest eyes or was the funniest, that sort of stuff. There were a few pages dedicated to descriptions of each of us, and Dalia's girlfriends were using a tape measure to record bust, waist, and hip measurements. I was attempting to keep a low profile so I wouldn't have to participate, but Dalia spotted me and came up to ask how I'd describe my nose, because it was her favorite and she wanted to put it in the book. I hated my nose just a little more than I hated the rest of my body. I was skinny but had a comical little potbelly, a couple of red adolescent stretch marks on my hips, and pointy boobs that I tried to hide by stooping and wearing loose T-shirts. My nose was an unusual shape without managing to be distinctive: a convex curve that, when I was small, I used to try to correct with Scotch tape. I thought it made me look nondescript. In fact, I felt nondescript in body and soul. Dalia, on the other hand, was notably gorgeous. She was tall, had a glowing brown complexion, perfectly straight black hair, shapely arms, white teeth, and a tiny, upturned nose. Her voice was deep, confident, and brisk, and she spoke in what sounded like a foreign accent but was in fact uniquely her own. She'd been born in Mexico to a Mexican mother, but her maternal grandparents—they died in a crash before her birth—were French, and she seemed to have inherited some of their linguistic mannerisms. Very few of the things said to me in those years had as much effect as Dalia informing me that she liked my nose. From that moment on, I looked up to her, although we didn't become friends until a few years later.

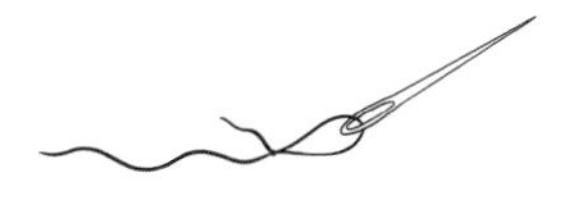

I learned to read and write at the same time as I learned how to cross-stitch. My grandmother had shown me the basics, but it wasn't until the workshop with Cristina in elementary school, when I was six, that I brought everything I'd learned together. Cristina was the least feminine of our teachers. She wore pants and plain T-shirts, no earrings or necklaces, and had very short, tightly curled black hair and small, almond-shaped eyes. Her voice was deep and soft, and she was invariably warmhearted and gentle. Her speciality was IT, but in her classes those of us who were also in her cross-stitch group (we were all assigned randomly to a craft class every three months: carpentry, cookery, traditional woodcarving, resin jewelry, pyrogravure, pottery, textiles, batik, or cross-stitch) were allowed to draw and design patterns using the zoom feature on the Paint program, which divided the computer screen into squares like the embroidery fabric. In that workshop, the reverse side of Cristina's pieces—which distinguishes the experts from the amateurs—was always an immaculate geometric pattern.

I still have the piece of embroidery I made in Cristina's workshop. It's a gray cat but looks more like a robot on all fours.

It seems late in the day to be introducing Dalia to my daughter; I went through this ritual with family and other friends ages ago. I feel awful that she's finally meeting her so long after everyone else, when she should have been one of the first. I'd also gone through that difficult period when it became clear which friends to keep and which to let go. The ones who understood the weariness, strange hours, and constant interruptions (many of them with children too), or who simply showed affection and interest in our new life, those who made no complaints about sitting on the floor to play while we chatted were on the "keep" list. The people who insisted on seeing us at truly inconvenient times, turned up with the idea of being offered food and drinks, and demanded as much attention as the baby have gone by the wayside. I'm scared that Dalia might turn out to be in the latter category. She never liked children. I'm so worried, I'd almost prefer not to put her to the test. Maybe she's changed, but I know very little about her life now. On social media, she posts only pictures of medieval manuscripts and articles on feminism and injustice. I have no idea if she has a partner, what music she listens to, what kind of clothes or shoes she wears, which songs she likes to dance to, if she even still dances. In the past, I'd known all those things about her. About them both. Or almost all.

Of course, another part of me is longing to see her again. I have so many things to tell and a great many more questions to ask.

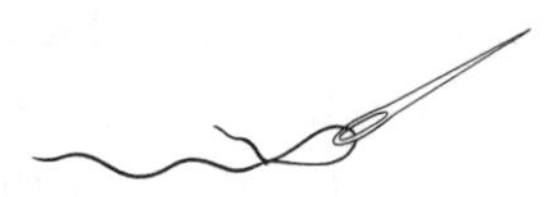

My grandmother Sofía was born in the Yucatán town of Maxcanú and moved to Mérida with her family at the age of twelve. She lived there until she married and came to Mexico City. She did little embroidery, the odd blouse with flowers in cross-stitch (*xokbil-chuy*, she used to call it) or a technique called *xmanikté*—a stitch that has been practiced in the Yucatán for centuries but is now in danger of dying out, despite the fact that the name means "forever alive." It's a very difficult stitch, using drawn threads to create a sort of brocade effect. It's often claimed that the Spanish brought needlecrafts to Mexico, but in the sacred cenote of Chichén Itza, archaeologists have found remnants of *xmanikté* dating from the pre-Hispanic era and other very similar examples of wrapped yarn work in the cave of San José de Ánimas in Durango State. The Chichén Itza relic is a piece of charred fabric with geometric designs. Small, open spaces were formed in the warp using needles made of bone or wood.

I once asked my grandmother to teach me *xmanikté*, but she said she was too tired, it was so complicated, maybe some other day. I didn't insist, and she never embroidered again.

The human body is made up of a number of tissues: adipose tissue, cartilaginous tissue, epithelial tissue, fibrous tissue, lymphatic tissue, muscle tissue, bone tissue, connective tissue.

Connective tissue consists of flexible, elastic threads woven in a delicate mesh that is very similar to silk. It unites the different parts of the body under the skin.

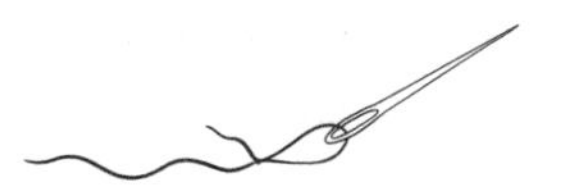

People always think a notebook will make a good present for a writer, but for me it's the worst. All those blank pages remind me how much I've erased and how little I've decided to keep, let alone publish. For months I've been trying to decide whether to give away or throw out the pointless collection of notebooks—their pages full, half full, or blank, like empty promises—that I've amassed in my desk over the past ten years or so. They pile up, collect dust. Even the used ones. I tend to think that at some moment I'll want to refer to my notes on art history or structural linguistics, or that I'll either enjoy myself or laugh—though more likely be ashamed—rereading the novels I attempted to write in college. I haven't done that once in the last decade and perhaps never will during my lifetime…or I might just reread them now. That's what I feel like doing. It drives me crazy to see the black, red, green, and blue notebooks piled there like panels in a ruined church, like small boxes of forgotten things, of failures.

It's been a long time since I've regularly carried a notebook. I take notes on my phone these days. In the past, I used to write by hand and absolutely never threw away museum or subway tickets. I found it satisfying, calming, exciting to document the discoveries of my life, the directions it took. But one day, life just seemed too short. I've hardly even had time to write in my daughter's memory book, only very occasionally jotting down some of the funny things she's come out with. Just a moment ago, it occurred to me to write something she said earlier today—Daddy has a lot of hands—but I got distracted when I rediscovered that journal from Europe.

Between the pages are the few photographs I took and the ones Dalia gave me. The first is of Dalia unpacking, sitting in a gray armchair in her cousin's minute apartment in London. It was so small that nearly all the furniture was foldable and stored under other things. We had a queen-size inflatable mattress that we could only lay out by moving all the other furniture in the bedroom to one side. The whole apartment, including the kitchenette and bathroom, had thick carpeting that had once been white but was now gray. It disgusted me to think of the body fluids, waste, and food that might be hiding in the pile of that carpet; the mold, bacteria, and insects living in luxury, reproducing and feeding on other molds, bacteria, and insects. I very quickly regretted not having brought my slippers and congratulated myself on having packed a course of antibiotics.

The cousin in question was a skinny man of about thirty with dark hair and heavy bags under his eyes. I thought he looked lovely. Dalia had to introduce herself because, although closely related, they hadn't seen each other since childhood. He was very attentive. We chatted for a short while, and he told us that he was about to go out to a nearby club and would be leaving for work early in the morning. He'd be back (very) late the following night and would then be away on a trip for a few days. He invited us to the club, but we were exhausted and fell asleep the moment our heads hit the pillow.

Dalia and I found ourselves wide awake at four the next morning. We lay in the dark for a while, chatting quietly, a drowsy conversation about how strange it was to be fully conscious at such an early hour. Dalia occasionally suffered from insomnia, and I asked about the techniques she used for getting to sleep. I recite "Suave patria," she said. What? I giggled. López Velarde? That's the one, she replied. It's a family thing. My grandfather had a bet with my mother to see who could learn the whole poem first. Your French grandfather? Yes, but when he emigrated he got more Mexican than tortillas. My mother used to recite it to me like a lullaby when I was little, and I ended up learning it by heart, so now I recite it to myself. Aloud? It still seemed hilarious. No, under my breath. What about you? What do you do when you can't sleep? I imagine I'm my aunt's cat, Orlando.

We eventually managed to doze off again. I woke before Dalia, by which time her cousin had already left. I hopped and skipped to the bathroom, trying to touch the floor as little as possible. It took me a while to figure out how to work the shower, and I came to the conclusion that this is the first sign of belonging in a place: knowing how to get hot water out of the shower.

For breakfast I had a little hard cheese and some sliced bread I found in the refrigerator, then settled down to read the entries in my *Lonely Planet* guide—I loved the name—about the places that, according to our detailed itinerary, we had to visit. Our schedule was tight because Dalia wanted to see as much as possible each day. What if we never go back to London? she'd asked when we were making plans. Of course we will, I replied, because at that age life seemed endless and the future radiant.

Dalia still hadn't awoken, so I used the time to find the router and check the new emails on my phone. There was a message from my boyfriend, Iván, asking about the flight and telling me that he was going to my friend Nadia's birthday party. I'd hardly been on the plane for half an hour when he was already emailing me. That felt both sweet and somehow unacceptable. I replied that we'd arrived safely, hadn't seen anything yet, but I'd tell him all about it when we did. I said I missed him. I wasn't certain how true that last part was because I was exactly where I wanted to be and with the person I most wanted to be with; all that was missing was to meet up with Citlali.

I also wrote to my cousin to ask if she knew a doctor who could help with Dalia's friend's abortion. When the doorbell rang to deliver my luggage, it took me some time to find the house keys and a while longer to work out how to use them. The noise woke Dalia, and when she got out of bed, she was already fretting: We were behind schedule. While she was getting ready, I asked if her cousin was gay—I wanted to rule out any kind of liaison with him, something I was torn between imagining and fearing. She said he most likely was; his parents were very conservative, and that was probably why Dalia had never heard the subject mentioned in her family, but he must be. I said I hadn't realized millionaire Mexicans lived in *cuchitriles* in London, and we wondered just how many times a millionaire you had to be in Mexico to be able to afford a European lifestyle, and then about what the etymology of that cozy-sounding word *cuchitril* might be. Dalia promised to look it up in her dictionary of Mexican idioms when we got back home—it wasn't, as I'd thought, a Nahuatl word, but came from Old Spanish, referring to a pigsty.

On the map in the guidebook, we'd marked the route to Bloomsbury in red. We had to take the underground to King's Cross, walk to Russell Square, and from there to the Charles Dickens Museum—circled on the map in Dalia's firm hand. We left the apartment, into which not a single ray of light had yet entered, and once outside were dazzled by the sunny blue sky and our excitement. At the first corner, we stopped to check the instructions painted in white on the sidewalk. Cars were passing in front of us, with their drivers on the right side of the vehicle. I told Dalia the story of a friend who had decided to try to drive in London and spent half an hour trying to get off a roundabout. Dalia told me about an acquaintance who hadn't taken the directions seriously and had been hit by a car, at which point I stopped finding it funny. We walked along arm in arm, keeping a careful watch on the traffic, which always seemed to be approaching from where we least expected it.

On the train, we talked about Citlali. Between our excitement and weariness, we hadn't really discussed the issue. Neither of us had a particularly convincing theory for what had happened to make her cancel her trip at the last moment. We'd been really looking forward to the three of us discovering London together and couldn't understand why she'd let us down; her spirits must have been as low as her cash flow, and, as always happened in such circumstances, she was digging herself into a deeper hole.

We got off the train at King's Cross and as we passed through the station, every sign we saw had us dreaming of the possibility of finding ourselves in Belgium, Amsterdam, or France in just a few hours. Just think how it would be if we had trains in Mexico that went to Colombia, Argentina, and Chile in no time at all, I said. Then we tried to figure out the right exit and which direction to take once we were outside. We failed. Dalia insisted on following the map; I thought we should ask for help. I don't know why you put so much trust in people, she said. How do you know they won't send us the wrong way? I responded by asking why she put so much trust in our nonexistent map-reading skills. We took the nearest exit and were faced with an imposing brick building with a clock tower topped by a blue spire. I persuaded Dalia that we should ask a woman in a green coat. She was very kind, but the directions she gave did, in fact, send us astray. Annoyed, Dalia wondered if all our days in London were going to consist of never getting anywhere. I remembered that phrase from Borges's *The Aleph*: "I saw a splintered labyrinth (it was London)," but didn't mention it because Dalia was already in a bad mood and didn't like Borges; she used to say that he was a dyed-in-the-wool old snob—I'd agree, but I secretly loved him. Anyway, the streets were splendid; there was nothing at all wrong with getting lost in London.

In the end, it was Dalia who suggested asking for directions again. A very patient man explained the route, and thirty minutes later we were in Russell Square. I was a little disappointed to see a small simple park with bare trees. I don't know what I was expecting: perhaps that I'd turn a corner and Mrs. Dalloway would appear with her fresh flowers, ready for her party; or Dylan Thomas would be there, reciting—almost singing, as he used to—"The force that through the green fuse drives the flower." Dalia took a photo of the plaque informing us that the members of the Bloomsbury Group had lived nearby, and we continued onward.

We almost lost our way again but managed to get back on the right track. And we loved Dickens's small brick house with its green door. Inside was the mirror in front of which the author used to rehearse his public readings, his couch, a window that had inspired some scene from *Oliver Twist*, and first editions of *Great Expectations*. I tried to hide how much all this moved me but failed. *Great Expectations* was one of my favorite novels; I'd learned whole passages by heart, like the part at the end where Pip, talking about Estella, says he sees "the shadow of no parting from her." Or my favorite part, when Miss Havisham tells Estella that love "is blind devotion, unquestioning self-humiliation, utter submission"; it is "giving up your whole heart and soul to the smiter." Dalia had only read *A Christmas Carol*, and that was when she was a child, though she remembered really enjoying it.

The highlight of the house was undoubtedly the commode: a carved wooden chair, the seat of which could be lifted to reveal a chamber pot. It made us wonder why contemporary toilets were all so alike, except for those Japanese ones that clean your butt with a jet of warm water and have heated seats in cold weather—Dalia said she'd used one in a sushi restaurant, but I didn't believe her. The only things Dalia photographed in Dickens's house were the commode and me standing at the green door on our way out.

We sat on the steps at the entrance to rest and decide what to do next. There was no time to visit another museum. We were hungry. Ideally we should find a supermarket to stock up on food for the apartment and save the cost of the very expensive London restaurants. Although truthfully I had no desire to save; I wanted to try out the restaurants, and, thanks to the legacy—that's how I thought of it—I'd unexpectedly received from my father, I had enough cash for at least the cheaper ones. But Dalia didn't, so I pretended to be in the same situation. Anyway, we were in agreement that we wanted to spend as little time as possible in her cousin's dirty apartment. We commented on the crumbs on the floor, the hairs in the carpet and the bath, and decided that we couldn't spend one more night there without giving the place a thorough cleaning. And that's how we passed our first evening in London. We found a small vacuum cleaner in a corner; we wiped over every surface and shook out everything shakable, imagining we saw cockroaches every few minutes until the lightheadedness that comes with lack of sleep and jetlag had us laughing our heads off. At nine o'clock we collapsed onto the mattress.

A cross-stitch alphabet sampler made by Anne Brontë has the following biblical quotation at the bottom: "It is better to trust in the LORD than to put confidence in man" (I imagine it refers to the whole human race and not just one man in particular). In Charlotte Brontë's novel, Jane Eyre sews as she watches her friend Helen being punished at Lowood school, and later in the novel she observes a woman sewing while being questioned about an attempted murder—Jane suspects the needlewoman of being the culprit.

Apparently, the Brontë sisters didn't like doing embroidery. They thought it was boring. In Jane Eyre's view, men and women have an equal need to make use of their abilities and suffer equally when they can't. She believes it's narrow minded to think that a woman's employment should be confined to domestic chores, playing the piano, and embroidery. There is, in her opinion, nothing laughable about a woman who wants to free herself of these restraints.

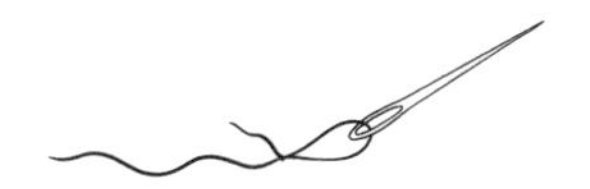

From my grandmother, I inherited a *Manual of Needlework for Ladies*, published in 1886. My grandfather had given it to her as a birthday present. I recognize many of the stitches: running stitch, backstitch, cross-stitch, hem stitch. Over the centuries the language of needlework has changed very little or has changed completely.

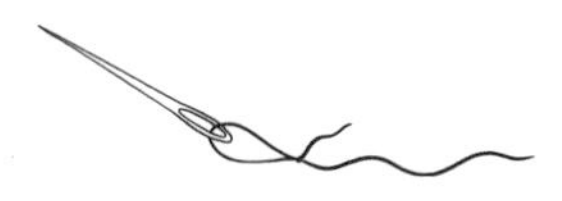

I don't know if our sex education classes were particularly poor or if it was that I heard only what I wanted to hear, because I'd thought menstruation just happened once and that was the end of it. They went on and on about "the time of the month when your period comes" without ever using the plural, so it didn't occur to me that it was going to continue on a monthly basis for the next four or five decades. My mother explained it to me when I was sitting on the edge of the bed, doubled up with stomach cramps. It's the womb rehearsing for the time when it has to push out babies during childbirth... you'll get used to it, she said. And rather than comforting me, her comment sounded sadistic.

It was the second semester of middle school. I'd exchanged my loose T-shirts with animal designs for plain black and sometimes red ones. In the evenings I read gothic novels—*Dracula*, *Frankenstein*, *The Monk*—and fantasy literature—*Harry Potter*, *The Wizard of Earthsea*, *His Dark Materials*. Then our English teacher gave us a story by Angela Carter, and I was crazy about its perfect mix of fairytale and the gothic, horror and eroticism that perfectly describes my feelings about transitioning from childhood to adolescence, although that idea only came to me later. Carter became my favorite author; I learned her stories by heart—they aren't so difficult to memorize, almost poems—and I filled my notebooks with drawings of her characters in red and black ink; I dreamed of being one of her implacable heroines: ferocious lady vampires, wolf women, seductresses. But the reality was just the opposite: I was a timid, inquisitive bookworm, more like a minor character from some story by Carson McCullers, whom I'd also begun to read avidly.

My fanatical love of Angela Carter involved a degree of ambivalence because I detested the teacher who introduced us to her work: an arrogant egomaniac and unprepossessing liar with a raw-fish complexion, a patchy balding scalp, and an equally patchy mustache. He used to humiliate the boys and flirt with the girls, and he was always spreading gossip and creating intrigue. But the moron had good taste. However hard I resisted, I ended up loving Edward Gorey, Coleridge, and The Clash. Just to make things harder, my family made me feel a little ashamed of my Anglophilia. My parents read Eduardo Galeano and listened to Salif Keita, Mercedes Sosa, and Cesária Évora, and during the best years of their marriage they would sit in the living room for hours playing *son jarocho*, even sometimes attempting to dance to it. That was what I felt I should like: folk or protest music, not my gringo songs. I liked my parents' music too—a little and in short bursts—but I couldn't escape my obsession with the soft, dark melodies of Björk and Alanis Morrisette because they were singing to me, or that's how I felt then.

Citlali used to ask me to summarize the stories of Carter, Henry James, and Neil Gaiman that we were assigned in the English class; she rarely felt like reading them herself. She was a very selective and slow reader, managing only one chapter at a time—she hated books without chapters. When I liked a book, I'd recommend it to her, and if my summary caught her imagination, she'd add it to her very long—stretching over pages—reading list. She used to say that before she died she'd make a will that, along with her other possessions, left her list to be shared among her friends. But she was always reading something, even if slowly, and she was always inventing stories she thought could be turned into movies or books.

For a few months, on Thursdays after class, Citlali and I joined a creative writing workshop lead by a former student, now studying literature. In one of the first classes, he asked us to work in groups to write the opening chapter of a possible novel, and we came up with an idea that had us hooked. *Adriana's Thread* was the story of a girl who inherited from her grandmother—a sort of witch—the magical thread that had belonged to Ariadne, the character in the Greek myth of the labyrinth and the Minotaur. When Adriana set the ball of thread rolling, it would lead her anywhere she wished. For example, if she said, "Take me to my friend's killer," she only had to throw the ball to the ground and it would roll straight to the feet of the guilty party. The workshop leader loved it, and since we loved him—he wasn't exactly good looking, but not ugly either, and was very smart and kind—we were doubly excited. Commenting on what we'd written, he was the first teacher to point out that the words "text" and "textile" had the same root: the Latin *texere*, to weave, braid, or compose. Citlali and I saw ourselves developing our novel into a movie and using the millions we earned to buy a yacht that we'd moor in Venice—where the two of us would live—and from there sail to every port in the world. A few months later, the teacher was awarded a scholarship to study in the United States, and the workshop came to an end. We were a little depressed by that but went on writing the novel with the idea of mailing it to him when it was finished.

Time passed, and we made a new group of friends, just as weird as the others but much more likeable. There was the blue kid, who always had one side of her head shaved, which gave her scalp its blueish tinge; we never dared to ask her why she did that—it didn't seem that she liked it that way, and there were rumors of cancer, operations, or skin problems—but her hairstyle was as punk as her nerve and genius for contradicting our teachers in class. She embraced the nickname when other students started using it to tease her. And then there was Libia, who was very tall and a compulsive liar, but in a good way because her stories were hilarious. Mara was a sort of cheerful human koala bear; she hardly ever spoke, but when she did it was always in beautiful, short, enigmatic phrases that sounded oracular. In addition, there were the two Matíases (Fernández and Undurraga), who dressed in black, made spectacular drawings of dragons in their exercise books, and did role-playing games during recess. Physically, they were very different, one fair and the other dark, but they were kindred souls. In the evenings, we'd all meet to go to a movie theater, study, watch some show on TV, or listen to music.

When Citlali and I were alone after classes, we'd shut ourselves up in her bedroom to eat cream-filled Miguelito pastries or handfuls of Lucky Charms cereal and listen to albums, discussing and memorizing the lyrics. I remember how excited she was by every word of "Tonight, Tonight"; she was, to my incredulity, in love with Billy Corgan, with his nasal voice and skull-like head: pale, bald, and rounded, just like, in my view, the main character in *The Nightmare Before Christmas*. Citlali used to say they weren't the least alike, that Billy Corgan's face was moon shaped.

Heaven knows what we were seeking in those songs: a particular mode of expression, of imagining; a collection of metaphors and stories; fragments of a vital lover's discourse to describe ourselves, to inhabit, exist, and feel in the world. Those songs, with their platonic loves and beautiful depressions, were a poor education for that world. It took many years, several disappointments, and innumerable cretins to rid ourselves of them, and it's questionable whether we ever really did: I still get emotional listening to that music.

When Citlali was five years old, her mother, who had a heart condition, died, and then she lived alone with her father. She'd often wanted to move in with her grandmother or aunts—the women who offered her the affection that kept her going—but her father wouldn't allow it. She used to say her grandmother was a good-hearted, happy person who adored and cared for her until she passed on when Citlali was eleven. We stayed with her aunts a few times; they were delightful, amusing, ironic, and loving. I hated her father: a tall, coarse, ill-mannered man who spat in the street, smelled bad, and never missed a chance to make Citlali's life hell. He'd shout at her, call her stupid, neurotic, a waste of space, and in the next moment be tender—too tender, I thought, disturbingly tender. Once, from the hallway, I heard him shitting, accompanied by what sounded like a grunt of satisfaction. From then on his body odor, his mere presence, made me want to retch. But even so, I preferred Citlali's home to ours because her father was employed in the offices of a dairy company, where he had to work until pretty late into the evening. At four in the afternoon Leticia—a heavenly cook with beautiful eyebrows who looked after and pampered Citlali, and was lovely to me too—left and we were alone. In my house, on the other hand, there were always too many people and too little space.

After my mom and dad divorced, we moved in with my grandparents, and I had to share a small, twin-bed room with my mother. I felt embarrassed about bringing my friend there, subjecting her to the constant interruptions, when all we wanted was to be alone and share our secrets. Citlali had a large bedroom with a big bed. She used her threadbare childhood blankie as a throw, saying that to get a good night's sleep she needed either that or a glass of whiskey.

The Adriana novel was progressing slowly. We bounced ideas back and forth, but apart from the central premise, nothing was really clear. That, however, didn't discourage us; we turned over possible subplots and imagined secondary characters: monsters, villains, and companion creatures.

Dating still didn't interest us, although we were constantly falling madly in love with boys at school, the ones who were least likely to notice us or even be aware we existed. I developed a crush on a boy I saw in the mornings from my mother's car, standing outside another school. That's when I discovered that if you set your mind to it, you could choose whom to fall in love with, could become enamored with almost anyone, especially if they were total strangers you could idealize.

We had a sex education teacher who once explained the different techniques of male and female masturbation. She said that women in particular had plenty of options: stroking and caressing yourself, rubbing your thighs together. Afterward, a rumor went around that the teacher had continued to discreetly rub her sturdy, crossed thighs under the desk for the rest of the class. I associated masturbation with the image of that woman: her rabbit face, long false eyelashes, and thighs in constant motion. So I didn't do it. The only orgasms I had were in my sleep, when I dreamed of the boy I saw in the mornings showering me in kisses in the middle of the street.

I began to hear that some people thought I was good looking. In the mirror, I could almost make out a sort of harmony in my features, the contrast between my black hair and pale skin, something attractive in the proportions of my new body, but it was as though I were looking at someone else, as though that beauty didn't belong to me, wasn't mine, since I'd done nothing to earn it; it was just a genetic coincidence that my appearance happened to correspond with the tastes of the time (misogynist, racist times, I now understand, but only vaguely suspected then). Desirability was uncomfortable; it was interesting, disturbing, and frightening all at once. I was immediately repelled by the boys who sent messages through friends saying that they liked me or thought I was attractive, but I wanted them to go on liking me, finding me attractive. So I started trying to be that person in the mirror, choosing clothes and hairstyles that would make her more desirable, but at the same time more aloof and unattainable.

As my mother flatly refused to buy me deodorant (it's carcinogenic) or razors (they cause skin irritation) just to please a bunch of brainless halfwits—her description of boys my age—I used to steal those items from my grandparents. When we were given permission to leave school to visit the shopping mall across the street during our free hour on Tuesdays, my week's allowance went on low-cut T-shirts, padded bras, deodorant, and razors. Mom advised me to scowl in the street and hide one hand in the sleeve of my sweater, pretending to be an amputee, so men wouldn't bother me.

One day, I actually met my platonic morning love. Our friend Libia, who had moved to his school, invited me to her birthday party, and there he was. He turned out to be a moron. The first thing he said was that I was lucky he was even talking to me because it was always the girls who started flirting with him, not the other way around. He then told me that his neighbor was the drummer—or maybe bass player—of Café Tacvba, as if that implied some form of musical talent on his part. I have no idea why I agreed to go to the movies with him the following day. Out of curiosity, I guess, or to be able to say that I'd had a date. Apparently (so he told Libia), he spent the whole time asking me to kiss him, but he was whispering and the soundtrack was loud, so I didn't even realize he was speaking. I could see that he was looking at me intensely and just smiled back from either perplexity or nerves. He found what he mistook for shyness charming. After that date, he began ringing our landline obsessively, but I didn't want to see him again. I thought my grandfather would scare him off because whenever the phone rang, he'd answer by trying to guess the caller ("Magnolia!"; "Banamex Lady!"). But the boy kept on pestering me for another date, and I kept on saying that it wasn't possible. One evening, I answered the phone, and he moved the handset close to a stereo playing Café Tacvba's "Las Flores." I felt guilty when the song ended, and I asked him to stop calling, said I'd look him up after the exams. I never did, but "Las Flores" became one of my favorite songs.

Around the same time a friend of ours, Matías Undurraga, also developed a crush on me. We'd gotten to know each other well because we had adjoining desks. Although fun to be around, I didn't find him the least bit attractive: he was sweaty, even on cold days, and his nails were too long—Citlali said that long nails on men were a sign of drug addiction, as they were used to snort cocaine. He wrote me a poem using my full name—no one called me Mílada; I was known as Mila—but forgot the accent on the *i*. When he declared his feelings for me, I was angry. I felt it was a betrayal, that our friendship had been a sham. I didn't know how to explain just what that betrayal consisted of, maybe that he was more interested in my body than in me as a person, or that he was willing to risk breaking the bond we'd forged for a passing, less stable sort of relationship. I told him that I wanted to be his friend at some point, but for now even that felt uncomfortable. A couple of months passed, during which I was completely frozen out—Matías Fernández wouldn't talk to me either—until we were told to change desks. That's when we became friends again.

At parties I never danced salsa. It was something only Dalia and a few others (the ones who also knew about sex, we assumed) were able to do. Citlali drank very little, except when she set out to get drunk, and then she went for the gold. On such occasions, our friend Mara's older brother, who was in high school by then, used to take advantage of the situation to shut himself away with her in one of the bedrooms. There were rumors about what happened between them, but nobody knew for sure. Citlali would never discuss the matter, although she did assure me that she was still a virgin and wasn't really keen on him, or only when she was drunk. I didn't believe any of those assertions.

Even the idea of getting drunk frightened me. I hated the thought of losing control and ending up kissing Matías Undurraga. I used to pour myself glasses of water and pretend it was neat vodka, and the minute people started dancing to reguéton I'd leave without saying goodbye.

My mother had an arrangement with a neighbor—a cab driver—to pick me up from parties at the stroke of midnight. He was a pleasant man who said little, so I'd listen to music on my headphones during the ride home—Citlali said this was very bad manners, but I didn't care. Those nocturnal drives, the headlights, reminded me of early-morning journeys to Acapulco with my parents when I was little. Even now, when I'm in a car after dark, I feel like I'm setting out on a journey.

A number of contemporary artists have employed samplers and other forms of embroidery to write feminist slogans that often contrast with the design and the ideal of the feminine in which needlework is pigeonholed.

Kate Walker (capitals on muslin): WIFE IS A FOUR-LETTER WORD.

Catherine Riley (white on white): SEX.

Tracey Emin (appliqué on a tent in various fonts and colors): Everyone I Have Ever Slept With 1963–1995.

Jean Chevalier and Alain Gheerbrant's *Dictionary of Symbols* says that in Islam, a loom "symbolizes the structure and motion of the universe." And even in the most remote areas of North Africa, the woman of each household possesses a basic loom consisting of two uprights and two wooden rollers. According to the authors, these are known as the "heavenly" and "Earth" rollers, thus symbolizing the entire universe. When a weaver completes a piece of cloth, she snips the threads attaching it to the loom while saying the same blessing the midwife gives when she cuts a baby's umbilical cord. The entry goes on to say that the thread and cloth are symbols of fate: The Moon weaves destiny, just as the spider weaves its web. The Fates are weavers.

I open a blue notebook—I'm going to open all of them—and come across a few paragraphs from the Adriana story I wrote with Citlali. In her room, perched on the edge of the bed or flopped on cushions, we'd argue, make notes, and then, back home, write our respective parts. Later, we'd exchange our first drafts to edit and modify what the other had written. We didn't get very far but did manage the opening chapters and also the ending, in order to have a clear idea of where the plot was headed. That was J.K. Rowling's system, I told Citlali, and it had worked for her.

In that drafted ending, Adriana used the magic thread to discover the identity of and capture the murderer of her friend, Ana. At that time we didn't even notice that the two names—Adriana and Ana—rhymed, and it wasn't until much later that it occurred to me that there was something symbolic in the coincidence, because Ana would go on existing in Adriana's memory, would be contained in it. Or it could also be read as the opposite, because when Ana died, a part of Adriana also vanished. At that time, Dalia and I had yet to become friends. It's impossible for me not to think about our names now: Mílada is an almost perfect anagram of Dalia. We used to joke that only an *m* stopped us from being twins.

Citlali wasn't totally convinced by the ending. Although it seemed the only possible one, she kept turning over other ideas; she wanted it to be happy, and the one we had definitely wasn't, because after justice was done, in that first moment of calm, in the instant of certainty that the murderer would never return to harm any other woman, Adriana felt a great sorrow being unleashed within her, spreading through her whole body. It was a sweet, icy sorrow: She finally had time to grieve.

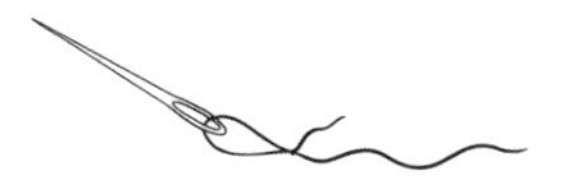

There are a couple of lines in Ovid's *Metamorphoses* that go something like this: Grief brings great inspiration and ingenuity outwits disaster.

I've never, and will never, read one of those books on how to write fiction, but it occurs to me that a novel could be written based on the instructions in needlework manuals, taking the following statements as if they were wise, disinterested pieces of advice:

"When embroidering the foundation, always use a sharp needle."

"Don't pull the thread too tightly; if you do, the loop becomes narrow and the effect is lost."

"Do exactly the same but in mirror image, reducing by one line at each step."

"When you stop embroidering, the work should be taken from the frame to allow the cloth to breathe."

The journal of the European trip is full of indecipherable jottings. I can't remember who Joseph Leonard was, why I wrote *National Geographic*, or even where I found this, in quotation marks: "He was a perfectionist." I imagine it has something to do with another note, which I do understand: "Walpole, Strawberry Hill."

On the third day of the trip, I woke at six in the morning, when Dalia was still sleeping. I showered, dressed, and read for a while in the bathroom so as not to make noise. In my inbox, I found a short, loving email from Iván and again felt a mix of tenderness and revulsion. I decided to wait until that evening to reply.

I was doing my embroidery and listening to Lhasa de Sela on headphones, so I didn't hear Dalia getting up until she opened the bathroom door. With the strains of "El Desierto" in my ears, I watched her approach, still half asleep. She leaned over my embroidery, then gazed at me, the marks of the pillow still on her cheeks, her eyelids puffy, and a confused expression on her face—even so, she looked lovely. What's that? she asked. I felt silly sitting there with my black-on-black embroidery. I'm the only one who can see what it is, right? Looks that way, she replied with a smile and then changed the subject, talking about our itinerary for the day: We were—predictably—already behind schedule.

We left the underground station and, for a long time, followed in the footsteps of a woman walking a small dog on a red, diamante-studded leash. I was telling Dalia that I thought I was capable of loving any person, or not loving them, but definitely capable of caring for them. If I got to know someone well enough, I ended by feeling some kind of affection for them, even if they were awful. Dalia didn't agree: Some people are downright hateful and that's fine—it means we can love the loveable people more, and much better. But when you say you're bisexual, doesn't that imply just what I'm saying, that you can fall in love with anyone, whatever their gender? No, just the opposite, she said. There are certain human beings I like because of an intellectual bond, physical attraction, chemistry, and that goes deeper than whether they have a penis or a vagina.

The library in the British Museum was closed for renovation. Standing outside the door, trying to see through, we were almost in tears. That's where Marx wrote, said Dalia, pointing at nothing. And Virginia Woolf, I added. No way.

In the museum, we separated: Dalia was keen to go to Egypt, and I wanted to see the chessmen from the Isle of Lewis—a medieval set in which all the pieces have expressions of either astonishment or boredom. We planned to meet again a few hours later at the tables in the lobby.

On my way to the medieval section, I decided to stop at the pre-Columbian room, which looked attractive from the outside: low ceilings and as dark as a cave. I was fascinated by pre-Hispanic cultures, particularly the Maya, perhaps because of their jungle iconography—jaguars, queztals, and the shadow serpent of Chichén Itzá—but also because it was to some extent still my grandmother's world. *Xmanikté* embroidery was a demonstration of all the small and huge things that had survived the Conquest and the rise of capitalism. I wished Dalia were there to ask by what twists of fate those spectacular pieces had ended up in London. It was the sort of odd fact she'd know, had memorized, like the surnames of all her classmates from kindergarten to college.

I stood for a time, contemplating the feathered serpent and the skull encrusted with gemstones. They were out of this world. The skull was inlaid with bands of turquoise mosaic; the white teeth gleamed as brightly as the two circles of white conch shell around the eyes, and the nasal cavity was lined with red, thorny oyster shell. The eyes were two convex mirrors of bright pyrite; I could see myself reflected in them, like a tiny shadow.

The label said that the skull represented Tezcatlipoca, one of the principal gods of the Mexica pantheon. Tezcatlipoca is he who knows hearts—continued the text—the smoking mirror. Those two phrases—the sound of them—bounced around inside my cranium: he who knows hearts; the smoking mirror.

Near the skull was another exhibit: a black magical mirror that had been brought to Europe after the Conquest and had come into the hands of John Dee, an alchemist and mathematician at the court of Elizabeth I. Dee used the mirror to conjure up spirits—he was trying to communicate with the angels and speak with them in the original language from before the Fall. It was also associated with Tezcatlipoca, the magical god of the smoking mirror.

In the eighteenth century, the mirror belonged to Horace Walpole, a romantic novelist in the gothic tradition and author of *The Castle of Otranto*. (In addition to his literary castle, he had a real one in Strawberry Hill, near London, which gave rise to the Gothic Revival style of architecture.) On the back was a handwritten quotation from Samuel Butler's 1663 poem "Hudibras" about a mirror that could be used to communicate with the Devil.

I left the room and walked along the passages, unable to focus on any other pieces. I wanted to discover more about what I'd seen and then immediately sit down to write about it all. Citlali would have loved the stories of the black mirror and the god Tezcatlipoca who knew hearts. And imagine how useful it would be to have a god like that as an ally! But you'd have to pray to it, and no one had ever shown me how to do that.

The medieval room was closed for renovation too, so I went in search of Dalia in Egypt but couldn't find her. I wandered around the mummies for a while. They were as stunning as she'd said—in particular the cats, who looked as if they were wrapped in dried palm fronds, with that stripy pattern all over their bodies and the eyes marked by simple, cute brushstrokes. As there were no alarms or ropes, I was able to get as close as I wanted to the mummified bodies. Beside me, a little boy was even touching a mummy's nose, without anyone scolding him. I hesitated to say anything, just in case it was some British custom.

At that moment, I became aware of my weariness, my leaden feet. There was still an hour to go until I was due to meet Dalia, but I made my way to the lobby and lay down on a bench. The echoes of the footsteps and voices of other tourists dispersed into in the open spaces of the white building and I fell asleep, clutching my backpack. Dalia gently shook me awake.

We went in search of something to eat. Dalia was tired too. I asked if she'd visited the pre-Columbian room, and she said she hadn't. I didn't have the energy to tell her all I'd seen; we were both suddenly extremely grumpy.

That night we went to a pub to meet Iris, my friend from college. Six of us were crowded around a rectangular table in a booth: Iris, Iris's boyfriend, another friend of hers (Laura), Eduardo (the lecturer who'd been on our flight), Dalia, and me. I sat next to Iris's friend, a young farmer who lived in the English countryside. She told me about her days among the sheep, close to Dorset's Jurassic Coast and its indomitable sea. PJ Harvey sings about the cliffs, she told me, then showed me photos of the landscape and her flock, naming each of the sheep—all Disney characters: Daisy, Wendy, etc.—and describing their individual personalities and habits. The sky was gray in almost all the photos, and Laura explained that England has an island climate, which is to say the weather changes without warning several times a day. One minute you're walking in the sunshine, and the next you're running through a downpour. That's maybe why the English are so phlegmatic, she said; it's a way of combating the unpredictability of the climate. I didn't really understand much of that idea, but there seemed to be a logic in it. I thought I'd like to live the way Laura did, with all the rain, mud, and wide-open skies.

Dalia was chatting with Eduardo, and you could see a mile off that he was under her spell. Everyone fell in love with Dalia after a half-hour conversation. I often asked myself how that happened and used to study her, noting her smile, the laugh lines around her eyes, the physical contact she established from the very start—a hand placed confidently on a forearm or wrist—that gave a sense of security and was never intimidating. But all that would have been nothing without her eloquence, the speed at which her mind worked. It wasn't merely that people wanted to have sex with her—although of course that came into it—they became obsessed, were mad about her. They gave her handicrafts, left fresh dahlias on her desk, secretly followed her home, wrote her disturbing letters, bad songs, and even worse poems. And then there were the people who loved her in silence, worshipping at her feet. I was unsure if I liked that kind of power over people—was unsure of how real that power was if it ended by exposing you to uncontrollable craziness and violence—but would have liked to experience at least a little of it. I wanted to emulate her, see what it felt like to be so electrifying, if only for a moment. But so far I hadn't been able to muster the courage to break things off with Iván. I fantasized about him leaving me: I wanted my freedom without the burden of guilt.

Between sips of cider, I made a secret bet with Iris that Eduardo wasn't going to have any success with

Dalia. In class, with the microphone and the stage setting, Eduardo might even seem attractive—all that reciting poems by Wallace Stevens and Vallejo from memory and his timid, melancholy personality had their charm—but here, sunk into his seat, his cheeks flushed and looking a bit sweaty due to the crush, he wasn't at his best. And then he had that strange mannerism: scratching his ear in just the same way as my aunt's dog did. I felt sorry for him. My negativity was also based on the fact that he was friendly with that awful high school teacher who had introduced us to Angela Carter. I'd seen them walking together in the corridors of the university (and had hidden so as not to have to say hello). On the other hand, Eduardo was also a friend of a professor I adored—Miguel Cordero—who was a young, personable anarchist, pessimistic but brimming with enthusiasm. He recited Chaucer in Middle English, *Beowulf* in Anglo-Saxon, and made my ears go bright red whenever he noticed me or asked me a question in class.

I won the bet. Eduardo's seduction campaign came to nothing. And I was glad. Just before midnight someone rang the bell and shouted, "Last orders!" We made hurried goodbyes and ran to the underground station.

Our time in London was too short to include Strawberry Hill. I talked it over with Dalia, but the itinerary was already full. There was just that entry in my journal to remind me to visit the mansion the next time I was in England.

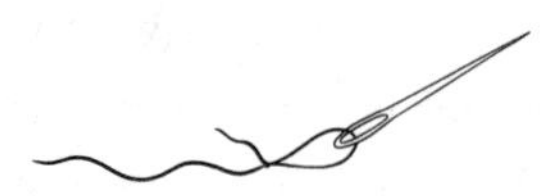

The oldest known example of a surgical suture is on an Egyptian mummy. The idea of being able to sew both fabric and skin must have been intuitive, a simultaneous discovery due to the likeness between the materials.

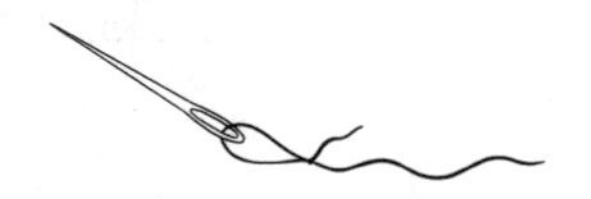

Recently, I've been coming across scenes of embroidery everywhere. For instance, in Elena Garro's novel *Los recuerdos del porvenir* one of the characters, Ana Moncada, is seen embroidering on a number of occasions. She's thinking with nostalgia about natural disasters. If only we could have a good earthquake, she says, and stabs her needle angrily into her work.

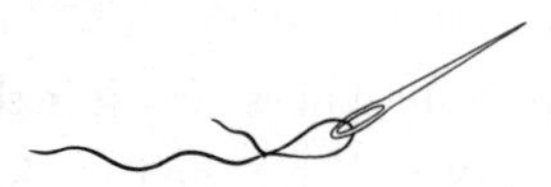

I clicked on Citlali's Facebook page in search of interactions, messages showing love or friendship, in an attempt to work out which of her *friends* really were friends. Then I made a provisional list of people to be invited to the leave-taking ceremony, including those living abroad who might want to send a letter or a video.

On Citlali's wall, there were several of those comments that speak to the dead person as if her soul were trapped somewhere in all the zeros and ones. Our middle school friend Mara, whom I hadn't seen since, but who had kept in touch with Citlali, had written, "You'll always be in our stories and in our smiles. You'll always be in me." There was also a friend who hadn't heard the news and had posted a photo of a tapir: "Lalis, I saw this and it made me think of you," the message read in English. "How are you? If you come back to Manaus soon, we'll go looking for them again."

Don't hang out with those rotten apples, the middle school principal told me one day. I can't remember why I was called to his office, maybe just for him to say those words, to tell me I was a good student but he didn't like my friends: Citlali, Mara, and the others. He was sitting behind his desk, fiddling with his long mustache; there was a small sand pit alongside the desk containing a sad-looking tortoise with a fungal infection. The potential I was showing would be at risk if I allowed myself to be dragged down the wrong path, he added. I said nothing, simply waited a few seconds in silence until he told me I could go.

After that interview, I was even more keen to hang out with them until they left school or, rather, were kicked out for poor grades or causing trouble. The incoming class for high school was much smaller, and our group of friends dwindled at the end of the academic year. Citlali and I were the only ones left. Plus Dalia.

The summer before starting high school, Citlali volunteered for a community adult literacy project. A group of students from a number of private academies met after class in our school to organize basic literacy drives in remote towns and villages. There was a six-month pre-campaign period, when the students organized parties and raffles to raise funds. Their training consisted of reading and giving seminars on the work of the educator Paulo Freire (the trainers were people who had taught in previous years), and they polled the populations of villages and gathered the provisions they would need to spend the following summer teaching adults to read and write. The literacy tutors—we called them ABCers—were easy to spot at school: The men carried backpacks and had strange hairstyles, with long strands in unexpected places; the women wore embroidered blouses, huaraches, and had dangly earrings.

Within the hierarchy of the project, Citlali was one of the *tapancos*: volunteers who went along to help out, get to know the campaign, and decide whether they wanted to join it the following year. They didn't need to do any training and were in the village for just one week as observers and teaching assistants. Citlali tried her best to persuade me to join her, but my mother asked me to go to the beach with her and my aunt, and I opted for the sand and sea. So Citlali went alone, although not really alone, because Dalia was there too. I couldn't figure out why Citlali would want to go off to work somewhere—I'd heard it was hard work—instead of staying home doing nothing, reading, listening to music, or binge-watching shows.

That summer, my mother and I moved into an apartment where we each had a bedroom—a room of her own. Mine caught the sun, but I barely noticed at first, because it rained every afternoon in July and August. On one of those rainy afternoons, my grandmother died. I'd been acting the ungrateful granddaughter for several months: Her slowness, confusion, and constant anxiety were a severe test of my patience. I quickly got bored in her company, and I had to help carry her, sit her in her chair, and feed her. Just a few hours before she died, she asked us to dress her in her traditional Yucatán clothes: a *hipil*, *jubón*, and *fustán* (she called it a *pic*), all of which she'd hand-embroidered with flowers. After her death, I was overcome by sorrow and remorse, with no other desire than to lock myself in my room and watch *The Sopranos*, read Rosario Castellanos's *Balún-Canán*, and mope. Rosario Castellanos was born the same year as my grandmother, and her words reminded me of her. I'd traveled a few times with my mother and grandmother to the Yucatán town where Grandma grew up, with its vast open skies, impossibly blue cenotes, and ruins hidden among the ceiba trees, and so had mental images of that other world where she was transformed into our guide and translator. Despite the fact that Rosario Castellanos's novel was set in Chiapas rather than the Yucatán, it forced me to relive and reconsider those scenes.

In some ways, I enjoyed feeling miserable and thinking about Grandma. I enjoyed feeling something—anything—intensely and believing that I was no longer a child, because I finally knew what death was.

One week as a tapanco was long enough for Citlali to make friends with the ABCers and become involved in the web of romances and friendships in the Michoacán village they visited. When classes restarted, Citlali would chat with her new friends during recess, and on the weekends she went to their parties. She fell for one boy who was dating the most beautiful girl in the whole campaign. I asked how she'd gotten so close to those people in a single week. It was the way we lived together, she said. When you're with people in a totally new environment, even for a short time, you get to know them well. Get to really love them, too.

I began to have difficulty following her jokes, understanding the references. I had the feeling that she was bored with me and was seeking out Dalia's company more often to talk to her alone. Their former, slightly distant friendship had been strengthened by sharing the experience of the campaign. Dalia had taught Citlali to dance salsa, and they had both learned the art of wordplay. Citlali was an expert at double entendres, which made me even more suspicious about what went on when she shut herself away with Mara's brother. She used to laugh at me when I didn't get the innuendos; she cracked up the time I was with her and another of the ABCers and I asked them about a song that described a girl as *rica y apretadita*. Did it mean she was wearing a dress with a nice tight waist, like in a ranchero song? They couldn't stop laughing, but didn't explain the sexual connotations before dragging me over to other friends to make me repeat my question so they could laugh at me too.

I felt very alone during those months and deeply regretted not having volunteered as a tapanco. So I enlisted in the next pre-campaign sessions, which started in the middle of the academic year. Citlali and Dalia also joined up.

Every Tuesday, Citlali and I would go to the fast-food area of Plaza Coyoacán and always ate at the same dingy sushi bar, despite the fact that Citlali once found a piece of glass in her spring roll. In compensation, she was given a greasy tempura she had no desire to touch—on that occasion, as on so many others, I finished off her meal.

After lunch we'd return to school for the weekly literacy meeting. Lots were drawn and I ended up in the Home brigade, where I and two boys who'd never cooked or washed a single item of clothing in their lives were set the task of calculating such things as how much food and detergent we'd need for two months. I put my back into that pre-campaign period. I learned about the "generative words" for adult literacy and Freire's methodology for teaching reading and writing to 300 Brazilian workers in forty-five days, about his notion of literacy as a tool of "consciousness raising" that would produce capable, responsible human beings. I went to training sessions on how to make pan dulce, with the vain hope of giving workshops. I allowed myself to be charmed and intimidated by the campaign coordinators—older adolescents who'd been part of the program for a few years, who acted as our leaders, and made a big deal of the secrets their rank in the hierarchy gave them access to and their unquestionable self-invested authority. Individually, they were pleasant enough; as a group they were unbearably solemn. They were constantly telling us that we weren't going to Querétaro (a village near San Juan del Río) to dole out charity or save anyone, except maybe ourselves by understanding how privileged we were and opening our minds to other world visions. The tacit assumption was that if we allowed ourselves to be taken under their collective wing, after that longed-for summer we'd be better people.

I sold cookies, sold tickets for the fundraising parties, and at those parties, I sold beer from behind the counter. Although, in theory, the tapancos weren't allowed to drink during the parties, Citlali did sometimes get drunk and would spend the night with a ginger-haired boy we used to call Elmo—a college student who had once taken part in the campaign and still came to events. It was just like with Mara's brother: She roundly refused to discuss what happened between them and said she didn't even like him much. When Citlali wasn't planning to get drunk—she used to make the decision in advance—instead of going home at midnight, I went to sleep over at her house. She'd learned to drive, and her father used to lend her his old car, so on the way home we'd switch on the radio and let the songs on the most "pop" station act as an oracle. We'd ask about the boys we liked (I was interested in someone different every week and, to be honest, interested in none of them), the upcoming campaign, and our doubts about our career choices; the first song to be played after the question was the oracle's response. Question: Is Scorpion ever going to break up with his girlfriend? Answer: "La Tortura."

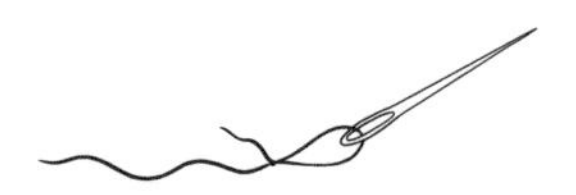

Before metal came into use, needles for suturing wounds were made of bone, and the thread was cotton or animal fibers such as tendons, muscle tissue, or horsehair. At one point in antiquity, the threads employed to sew skin were identical to those used for the strings of musical instruments.

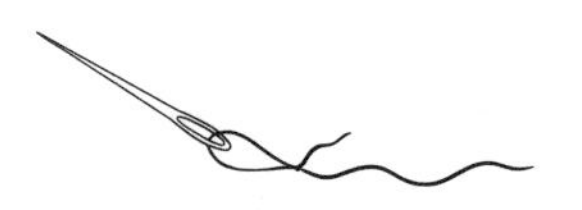

My Dear Friend—begins Dalia's message. How are you? How is your lovely family? I'll be in Mexico next week and I'd love to see you and finally meet that gorgeous daughter of yours. My time's a bit short because I'm coming for a conference, but how would Wednesday the 13th at ten a.m. work for you? I'll bring cookies. Let me know what you think. Hugs and kisses, Dalia.

"Hugs and kisses," she says. "My Dear Friend," she calls me. Never before have such tender words seemed so cold to me. I know it doesn't make sense, but I'm annoyed by, for example, the precision of "Wednesday the 13th at ten a.m." It's remained there, intact, unchanged over all these years: the sense that she doesn't love me as well as I deserve, the unfairness of me loving her so much more. The times I've gotten angry with her, the times I've deliberately hurt her, have all been the products of that feeling.

We'd spent three nights in London, but I still hadn't gotten over my jet lag. At six the next morning I was up and about before the sun, while Dalia was still lying on her back, snoring gently. She was so deeply asleep that I didn't have to creep around to avoid disturbing her, but the truth is that I wanted her to wake up, wanted to start the day as soon as possible. I demolished an apple in a few short, sharp bites and dressed without worrying about the noise my boots made—Dalia remained out for the count. Seven o'clock struck. The itinerary for the day was this:

Westminster Abbey 10:30 a.m.
Tower of London 1:30 p.m.
Charing Cross 5 p.m.

It hadn't occurred to us to plan our schedule in relation to the proximity of the places we wanted to visit; all that was going to require several underground journeys.

There was another email from Iván. I'd forgotten to respond to his last message but decided not to read this one yet and reply to them both that evening.

Dalia was now lying in the fetal position, her hair sticking up as if blown by the wind. In desperation, I decided to go out alone and left a note on the table saying, Gone for a walk! Be back soon, but if you want to set out without me, I'll meet you later at Westminster. And if I miss you, we'll catch up back here.

The light of the sun reflected on the white snow was almost blinding, and the cold air swept away my last shreds of drowsiness. I didn't know where to go. I was alone in London.

I boarded the underground at Mornington Crescent and got off at Waterloo—not so much from instinct as from The Kinks' song "Waterloo Sunset," which began playing in stereo in my head when I read the name of the station. I came out onto an uninteresting street but beyond some buildings caught a glimpse of that gigantic wheel of fortune, the London Eye, and walked toward it. The Eye was on our itinerary for a few days later, but I didn't care. I wanted to view London still blanketed in freshly fallen snow, in the morning light, and from high above. There was no line at the ticket booth, and I was the only person in my transparent pod. It was like being an astronaut. I was afraid I might suffer from vertigo, because the last time I'd been on a Ferris wheel,

I'd had a brief panic attack, but this one was so huge, moved so slowly, and the panorama was so splendid that I didn't even think about falling, just going up and up. The "dirty old river" looked brand new and clean to me; the tower of Big Ben seemed rather small; the spires of Westminster Abbey and the Houses of Parliament pierced the muslin of the air without tearing it.

When I arrived back at the apartment, Dalia was waiting by the door in her coat, visibly agitated. Where had I been? Why hadn't I woken her? I'd messed up the whole itinerary. No way was I going with her to the London Eye another day, it was too expensive to do twice, she'd have to find a space to visit it on her own. Standing in the doorway, she was looking at our schedule, trying to juggle the times. She wasn't mad with me, she said, just felt like it was all too much.

We were both irritated when we set out, but the annoyance dissipated quickly. It was our first experience of snow, apart from the grubby, compacted stuff we'd occasionally seen near Iztaccíhuatl and Ajusco. Dalia took off her gloves to touch it, picked up a handful and smelled it, put it to her lips and licked it. She stomped in a small drift. How long will it last? She asked. Is it going to melt? I hope not, I replied. We'd read that it rarely snowed in London, so we were lucky. Dalia took pictures, and we walked on arm in arm.

I'd assumed all the churches in the world were free, but the tickets to enter Westminster Abbey were really expensive. We stopped, our souvenir guides open, beneath the statue of the Virgin, then those of Martin Luther King Jr. and the other modern martyrs that had been commissioned in 1998 to fill the niches left unoccupied since the construction of the abbey. I wanted to see the tomb of the Brontë sisters. Dalia had no particular plan, so she tagged along. Passing between the display cabinets and memorial stones, we came across Darwin and Jane Austen. My beloved Jane Austen. I clutched the guidebook so tightly it somehow felt like I was hugging her ghost.

I told Dalia that even the thought of being buried gave me claustrophobia. Dalia agreed; she wanted her ashes to be thrown into the air from a mountaintop. Dalia was a climber; she and her mother took classes together and signed up for group expeditions to scale Mexico's mountains and volcanoes. She specifically wanted her ashes to be scattered from the top of Iztaccíhuatl so she'd become a part of that sleeping beauty. I suffered from altitude sickness and would begin feeling dizzy and nauseous as soon as I started an ascent, so my preference was for a garden, my ashes buried beneath a tree: a magnolia, a jacaranda, or a flame tree. Some place where people could go to remember me.

We stopped at Philip Larkin, and I had to stifle the desire to burst, right there and then, into a recitation of "This Be The Verse" or "To Failure." But I did recite them silently; Dalia asked where the lines inscribed on the stone came from: "Our almost-instinct almost true: What will survive of us is love." I couldn't immediately remember. I thought it was a poem about a tomb or something; the tomb of a nobleman and his wife—I suddenly recalled—who might even be buried in this very abbey. I bet, quipped Dalia. Seems like the whole world and their cousins are buried here. Where do they find space for the new ones?

It isn't a grave, just a monument, a Spanish woman standing nearby informed us. She'd just read it in her guidebook, she continued, showing us the green volume she had in her hand. He's buried in a cemetery. Lots of them are. Don't get the idea that they're all here.

We hurried on to the Brontës and discovered that it was a memorial too. We were already late for our visit to the Tower of London. I wanted to spend longer in the abbey, but I had no intention of annoying Dalia again that day.

Back on the underground, we managed to find seats together. My feet were killing me. We commented on how handsome English men were and how lovely the women looked. Then we talked about Citlali. I hope she comes back with us, I said. She'll starve to death in France. No, she should stay, responded Dalia. Mexico's not right for her. With that abominable father, I added, but maybe she could move in with her aunt or find a job and a place of her own. It's not that simple, said Dalia.

The Tower of London was enormous: there must have been at least forty of them, not just one. We joined a guided tour but slipped away after a while because we thought the arsenal was boring and our guide had little to say. What we wanted to see was the tower where Anne Boleyn had been imprisoned and the courtyard where she died. We started to walk in that direction, but on the way came across the crown jewels. Dalia wasn't interested. You had to buy another ticket, and, given all the damage mining had done to the world, she didn't get why people made such a fuss about seeing some plates and precious stones. She said she'd wait for me outside.

I went in briefly and returned to find Dalia on a bench surrounded by snow, embroidering the red flowers of her bookmark. I thought of Snow White's mother, that queen who pricked her finger while she was embroidering, watching the snow fall in the darkness and making a wish to have a daughter with hair black as the night, black as ebony, skin white as snow, and blood-red lips. Snow White was nothing like Dalia. My friend was much more beautiful. She was finishing off the flowers of the bookmark and, to cut the thread, took out an enormous pair of scissors: "poultry shears," she used to call them. She preferred them to Citlali's nail scissors (Citlali was able to make a straight tear in the fabric just using her hands) or my small, curved, stork-shaped ones because she could cut both the material and the thread with them. It used to make me laugh to see those big scissors being used on such tiny, delicate pieces of embroidery. I had the urge to just stand there for a while, watching her sew; it feels good sometimes to see what the people you love are like when they are alone. Not to spy, but to know them better. But there was nowhere to hide. I went over and told her how weird it had been; so many people visited the vault that you had to enter through an electronic beam and could only glimpse the pieces for a moment as you passed, like sushi in a trendy restaurant.

We thought the White Tower, where Anne Boleyn was kept prisoner, was the best part. There was old graffiti, scratched on the walls by people condemned to death, that made you feel you were voyaging back in time. You could still feel the nails digging into the stone, the superimposed ghosts of those hands.

On one of the upper floors, there was an axe and stone block, and in the garden below a guide showed us where the prisoners had been beheaded. On the spot where the executions took place, the grass was a suspiciously bright shade of green.

On our way out, we passed the ravens, eight huge birds that lived there and had to go on living there because otherwise, according to legend, the entire kingdom would fall. There was a monument to all the birds that had died since the 1950s, which instantly became my all-time favorite memorial. I asked Dalia to take a photo of me standing beside it.

We had one more stop on our itinerary but were shattered. All the seats on the underground train to Embankment were taken, so we stood chatting like flamingoes, shifting from one leg to the other to relieve the pain. We talked about the ravens, about how silly it was that Spanish has only one word for both small and large crows, while English distinguishes between them. We were silent for a while, and then I told Dalia that Iván's friend Pablo—a good-looking, slightly slow-witted medical student—was really into her. He'd seen her a few days before we left, when we were having coffee in a café in the center of Tlalpan, and had told Iván that he thought she was gorgeous. Dalia asked why I hadn't told her earlier since we'd been together for so many days. I didn't know how to respond; in fact, I didn't know why I hadn't when it would have been natural to pass on the comment immediately, to have called her just to share that snippet of gossip. Dalia thought the news was opportune since she was about to break up with Juan, a student of Italian literature who sent her love letters in Classical Latin, which, despite her not being able to read the language, still managed to enchant her. Everything had started brilliantly, but two months into the romance, she'd had enough. She'd decided not to say anything about the breakup before our trip but was going to tell him that she couldn't go on when she returned to Mexico. I thought you were getting along so well, I said, although I was secretly pleased because I thought Juan was obnoxious—he spoke like a book and was always correcting my syntax when we were talking: "That sentence should be in the subjunctive." He was a pain in the ass. Dalia said that, in fact, things had been lousy. He bored her, exasperated her, and she hadn't been able to tell the poor guy because he was going through such a rough patch—his house had flooded, he'd caught chickenpox, and he'd flunked two classes. And he made the most of those situations in such an unpleasant way; he lost all his sense of humor and was constantly crying and bemoaning his fate. He was such a drag; it got depressing.

We had little energy left for the bookstores on Charing Cross Road. When we entered the first one, Dalia immediately had an allergic reaction to the dust. I imagined her in the years to come, a renowned academic who began sneezing as soon as she put her nose inside a library. We sat on the floor in a narrow space between the shelves, each with ten books, deciding which to buy. Dalia opted for *Far from the Madding Crowd* and asked me what I thought of Hardy. I told her I preferred his poetry. She sneezed. I quickly decided to buy Sylvia Plath's *Ariel* and leafed through Ted Hughes's *Crow* and Doris Lessing's *Golden Notebook*. *Crow* is high on Érik's list of favorite books, said Dalia. Érik—one of her exes—had good taste in books so his recommendations were worth hearing. When we left, I had five books in my bag (including *Cat's Eye* by Margaret Atwood; I already had a copy, but the edition was beautiful) and Dalia had just one: Shirley Jackson's complete short stories—I'd managed to convince her that they were wonderful, which felt like an absolute triumph.

We'd planned to go to Foyles as well, but when

we realized how much farther it was, we changed our minds and returned to the apartment instead. Our itinerary mentioned only the street name: task completed.

There's a scene in *The Prime of Miss Jean Brodie* by Muriel Spark where a group of girls are in a needlework class, and as they sew, the teacher reads to them from *Jane Eyre*. Some of them try pricking their fingers to decorate the fabric with bloodspots.

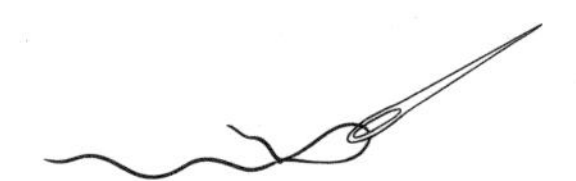

Citlali's Facebook page had photos of her: at the beach, standing on a sand dune with her arms raised; on the deck of a boat, wearing a windbreaker and with her hair curling in the sea air; selfies with a dark-skinned girl with a big smile and very white teeth. In the most recent—even that was posted months ago—she's standing by a mountain bike on a path in some rural setting, wearing a helmet and kneepads. I can't imagine her as an explorer; in middle school we used to spend P.E. at the ping-pong table while Dalia and the others were playing basketball, volleyball, or soccer. The teacher had by then lost faith in our sporting abilities and exempted us from all other activities. After a while, we got to like ping-pong and became good players, although never good enough to win the school championship. But we did almost win the domino tournament, because we entered without really knowing the game, and our strategies threw the other players off track, to the point where they yelled, I don't get it! You were playing sixes! How can you open with a two when you're playing sixes?

On the top left of the screen is the circle containing her photo: She's wearing one of those coarse, cotton, hooded shirts with stripes and diamonds that they sell in Coyoacán. The shot is taken in profile, with her eyes closed and her short hair ruffled. One hand and her lips are touching something that seems to be made of stone. When I double click to enlarge the image it turns out to be the head of a camel. Citlali always loved animals and children—loved them more than she did kisses, which she'd do all kinds of maneuvers to avoid, preferring to just shake hands with people. She used to say that she didn't want children, didn't want to add to the environmental catastrophe, but when she was living independently, she'd have lots of pets, something that was impossible at home because her father was allergic to cats and dogs. In the last year of middle school, she secretly adopted a cat: a stray gray tom that would sometimes sneak in through the school gates. She left food and water for it among the bushes near the entrance. She couldn't, however, work out a way to feed it during the summer break, and when we returned it had vanished. That was the same summer I had to miss the first week of the adult literacy campaign to accompany my mother on a visit to my great-aunt in the Yucatán. We agreed that afterward I'd go directly to Yospí, the Hñähñu village in Querétaro where the campaign was based that year. My great-aunt's house was on the beach, which convinced me to go. That and the idea of seven whole days with nothing to do but read—I'd been told there would be no time for books in Yospí.

The day I returned from the coast, a friend who was also going to Yospí gave me a ride. Or rather, her father, who was driving, offered to take my mother and me along. Mom was eaten up with worry and wanted to check for herself that our accommodations were safe. She was twice as worried when they drove home.

We were staying in an elementary school that was empty for the summer months. There was a central atrium where the women slept: twenty of us with sleeping bags and colored plastic storage drawers for our clothes. The rules about clothing were strict: It had to be loose fitting, and low necklines weren't allowed; brand logos, short sleeves, skirts, dresses, and shorts were also out. The idea was to attract as little attention as possible and so lessen the impression that—for want of anything better to do during the vacation—a pack of rich kids had invaded the village to amuse themselves among the local people. I had to change my usual outfits for the embroidered blouses my grandmother had made—the ABCers were always teasing me about them—and some that my mom and aunts had given me as presents. I'd hardly ever worn them before: Oaxaca blouses embroidered with running stitch, woven ones from Chiapas, and others from Veracruz and the Yucatán with cross-stitch designs. (I had no idea in those days that in the different types of embroidery, the signs and symbols can be read as the myths, historical events, and sociological elements of the various communities from which they originated, and was capable of seeing only the aesthetic and decorative aspects.) There was nowhere to do laundry, so we had to wear the same clothes for two or even three days until a cohort went to the laundromat in San Juan de Río—I almost came to find the smell of the second-day clothes pleasant, especially when compared with the third-day ones.

In my storage drawers, I kept a secret stash of candy and the eye mask and earplugs I wore to sleep; we had no curtains, and a tuneless chorus of snores accompanied the chirping of insects and howling of dogs each night.

On one side of the atrium was the kitchen area, where every morning the breakfast crew prepared burnt rice, cold oatmeal, and watery scrambled eggs with tortillas. The rule was that you had to finish everything, but I'd eat very little and sneak off later to gobble my candy and the María cookies and vanilla rolls I bought at the corner store on my way to the bathrooms.

And that was probably the worst thing about the place: To reach those bathrooms, you had to cross the schoolyard, and then go outside into the street to an adjoining room. At night, the concrete yard would be covered in incredibly inept flying cockroaches that hurled themselves without distinction at trees, headlamps, and anything walking. I've always had a phobia of flying animals; I love birds, butterflies, and bats when they are still, but if they flap their wings anywhere near me, I have to close my eyes and cover my face—it possibly has something to do with the balls whizzing around the schoolyard—so I got into the routine of not drinking water in the evenings and waiting until morning to visit the bathrooms. I used to set my alarm for five minutes before the coordinators woke us (usually with some joke, story, or song that no one found amusing) to avoid the line of people, come back, and quietly get dressed inside my sleeping bag—a series of contortions that needed practice and that I learned from the veteran ABCers.

There was only one shower, which we were allowed to use in same-sex pairs on alternate days, unless you were female and having your period, in which case you could shower alone daily. I'd never before in my life seen such a wide variety of naked women. There was every type of body: short, tall, brown skinned, pale skinned; big boobs with small nipples, or small boobs with large nipples. I loved the diversity of hips, thighs, shoulderblades, vaccine scars, moles, belly buttons, and feet, and it very soon felt normal to see each other in the nude, whether or not we were friends. Citlali often used to ask me to shower with her, mostly to avoid having to do it with Dalia, because she had a thing about her navel piecing. I thought it must be like my flying-animal phobia, invoking just a slight shudder, an involuntary reflex, but one day an ABCer with a tongue piercing—she was half in love with Citlali but wanted to get her goat—chased her to give her a lick with that pierced tongue, and I looked on as Citlali sobbed and trembled with atavistic animal fear.

Citlali and Dalia's bodies are the ones I remember best. I didn't shower as often with Dalia; we weren't yet true friends at the start of the campaign, but we liked one another and got along pretty well. We must have showered together two or three times, and though I've no idea what we talked about, I do remember her collar bones, like two letters sculpted above her broad chest—Citlali and I had rounded shoulders—her small, dark breasts, and her body under the flow of water: her skin was like damp wood—the smoothest wood that had ever existed—except for five or six bright stretch marks on either side of her hips. Citlali's body was always shivering with cold; her bones, clearly outlined under her pale, almost transparent skin, looked like they might pierce it at any moment. She had two dimples just above her butt that made her back resemble a face, a sad face in a blueish body.

When we'd finished showering, we mopped the floor, which was always flooded, and we had to clean the whole bathroom once a week, also in pairs. My partner was Citlali. We found that chore disgusting but used to laugh a great deal as we worked, trying to guess who the hairs—including pubes—belonged to as we sponged them up.

The men's sleeping area was at the back of the atrium. We never went over there, but through gaps in the curtains got glimpses of a miasma of sweat and earth and a tangle of dirty, lone socks.

Beyond that was the storeroom where, among the boxes of canned tuna, bottles of detergent, and packets of rice, there were cushions, a TV, and a DVD player. Only the coordinators had the key to the storeroom, and it was an open secret that they went there to make out. We hated them for having dominion over sex: Apart from those of us lucky enough to be dating a coordinator, we had to content ourselves with necking in our sleeping bags in the evenings, or in the storeroom when movies were shown on weekends. It was there that I first saw Dalia snuggling up with Bernardo. At the time, she was dating Érik, who was very smart, very funny, but neurotic. He was taking piano classes with the aim of studying at the music academy and, as he had to practice a minimum of three hours a day, had stayed home for the summer vacation. I was kind of friendly with Érik because we worked together in the physics lab. He was a disaster at math but used to keep me entertained with really good stories while I wore my brains out trying to solve the equations. I didn't admit it to myself at the time, but I now think I was a little in love. It made me angry to see Dalia cheating on him with Bernardo, not just for his sake but because she was doing it so blatantly that I had to make a choice between telling Érik or lying to him, neither of which appealed to me.

Then I met Iván, a tall, thin, dark-haired boy with a swimmer's shoulders and sad eyes. He was even good at math. Although shy, when you spoke to him one on one he had a great sense of humor and told brilliant jokes in a quiet voice without ever laughing. He was pretty much a loner and in his leisure hours used to read popular science, history, and philosophy—it turned out that there was, in fact, time to read during the campaign. Iván was giving classes near where my students lived, which in turn was near Citlali's, so it was his job to escort us to our afternoon sessions. On those long treks under the summer sun and clouds, along paths bordered by fields of tall maize, dodging puddles teeming with tadpoles, I began to feel attracted to Iván. He wasn't anything like the sort of man I thought I'd find attractive, but, on the other hand, he was just the sort of man

I thought would be attracted to me. I found him handsome in a way that wasn't immediately obvious, and I felt lucky, almost smart, to have discovered it. I finally fell for him one day when my students weren't home and I accompanied him to his class, where I watched him patiently explaining to his students how to do subtraction and challenging the children to see who could produce the best imitation of a gobbling turkey.

Citlali was, of course, the first to notice how much I liked him and didn't give up pestering us (separately) until she got him to admit that he liked me too. I was a little concerned about Citlali's reaction, worried that she'd feel she'd been set aside or abandoned, but she said she thought it was amazing and forgave me there and then for giving up on our plan of being a pair of old maids in Venice. She'd live on a boat on her own, and I could visit her with my dozens of children whenever I liked. It made her happy to think that two of her friends had a thing for each other and that we were going to stop hiding it. What had taken me so long? She teased me, invented songs, made hearts with her fingers whenever Iván turned to look at me. It was so over the top that I started to suspect her enthusiasm.

During the weekend movies, I'd arrange things so I coincidentally sat next to Iván and—casually—gave him my hand and leaned on his shoulder. Then one night we sat at the back and he kissed me. It was a bit of a let down. I'd expected his kisses to be softer, less slobbery, strange, and bitter—I later discovered that the bitter taste was his lip balm.

After a couple more determined, and more pleasurable, attempts, Iván told me that it was customary on the campaign to consider yourself formally dating after the third kiss. As it was his second year, I believed him. When lunch was over, in the time before we had to leave for our classes, we'd sneak into one of our sleeping bags and, snuggling up in the steamy air, explore every inch of each other's bodies. There was something addictive about going a little further each time: his hand gradually moving down until it reached my crotch and staying there, first for a second, then two, then a whole minute. We'd try to move as little as possible, make no noise, and I loved that: being in the darkness of the sleeping bag, silent, hardly stirring, focused on pure sensation. It was Dalia who, a long time afterward, explained that vaginal orgasms can give less pleasure than just kissing, than gradual, expert arousal.

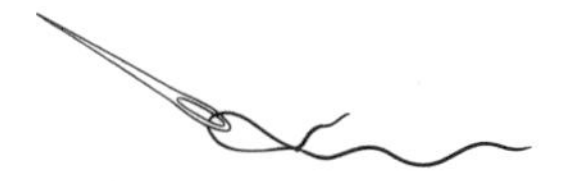

There's an Egyptian papyrus that describes what must have been an amputation. It says, "Treatment: Now after thou hast stitched it, thou shouldst bind fresh meat upon it the first day. If thou findest that the stitching of this wound is loose, thou shouldst draw (it) together for him with two strips (of plaster), and thou shouldst treat it with grease and honey every day until he recovers."

I tell Dalia that Wednesday the 13th would be fine by me, even though I have mixed feelings about it. The thing is that we've always had rather incompatible ways of expressing sorrow, and now, with Citlali's death, I'm afraid the meeting will be strained, soulless, that it will be proof of how far apart we've grown.

Dalia lives in Seville. I've often thought about visiting her there, but when that would have been a viable proposition I never got around to it, and then life became complicated. Traveling with a young child is no joke. It's impossible to keep my daughter quiet in a seat for even an hour, and that's only the first in a long list of difficulties. I try to avoid travel whenever possible.

During the Second World War, on February 15, 1942, Singapore fell to the Japanese forces. Whole families of the soldiers, doctors, nurses, and missionaries from Denmark, Australia, New Zealand, and the United Kingdom were taken prisoner. The women and children were sent to prison camps in Changi and the men to hospitals and nearby military camps. The female captives lived in horrendous conditions, but they were allowed to give classes in embroidery and quilting. Ethel Mulvaney had the idea of asking permission to make three quilts, one Australian, one British, and one Japanese (for the sake of appearances), to be sent to the men's camp. The authorities agreed. Each of the women had a square on which they embroidered flowers, words of encouragement, their names, and coded messages that let the men know they were alive and well.

The morning after my escapade on the London Eye, I woke up to find that Dalia wasn't in the apartment—it was so small, you only had to turn your head 180 degrees to check if anyone else was there. She was getting me back for my betrayal of the itinerary, but I didn't mind; I loved the idea of being alone for a whole day in

London, doing whatever I pleased. I was on the point of setting out when Dalia returned, shaking out her wet coat, wiping the soles of her shoes on the rug, and grinning from ear to ear. She'd been to the London Eye; the itinerary was intact, order had been restored, and she was satisfied. I was left open-mouthed, not having understood the strength of her need for symmetry and control. A mix of laughter, fondness, and pure bewilderment overwhelmed me.

For the rest of the morning, I observed her with a degree of objectivity. We went to see the Changing of the Guard at Buckingham Palace. Dalia took photos of the soldiers dressed in red and black—they looked like pipe cleaners—while asking me who'd recommended we watch that ridiculous ceremony. I couldn't remember, maybe an aunt or uncle—probably my uncle: the one who'd also said we should have tea and scones in some horribly expensive place and gave me money to treat Dalia too. I used his gift to buy a green button-down dress and then felt guilty because I'd already told Dalia about the scones. She was running short of cash; thanks to my miraculous paternal inheritance, I still had plenty. I was ashamed of my craving for new clothes; Dalia never wasted money on stuff like that. Her mother bought all her clothes for her, and she also wore things she'd inherited from her grandmother. Her outfits never matched, but she made it seem as though that was the whole idea, and her self-assurance gave her a lighthearted, carefree air. When I came out of the store with my green dress, I promised Dalia I'd take us all out for fondue in Paris. She wasn't the least bothered, just smiled and forgot all about it.

The itinerary next ordered us to Hyde Park, but there wasn't much to see there in winter. We walked around for a while among the bare trees—the skeletal oaks, planes, and silver birches. We said hello to a catatonic swan on the bank of the Serpentine, and it was there that I commented that Citlali must be dying of cold, because she'd decided to buy winter clothes in France so as to have less to carry. She'd been sure of getting work in some ski chalet in the Alps but hadn't yet found anything. Thin people feel the cold, Dalia agreed. Fat insulates you.

We strolled along pensively for a while, concerned about Citlali, and then a black and white magpie distracted us, returning our minds to the park. We tried to picture it filled with birds in spring, leaves appearing on the branches and buds on the point of bursting into flower. And then in summer, with so many different shades of green. Then with the blaze of fall colors. It was only possible for us to see the wild, leafy English gardens in our imaginations, because in winter they were just sketches, gardens of the mind. We spent half an hour in the park and then, our noses streaming from the cold, went to the National Gallery.

I'd done my research for this visit, had read guides, delved into the histories of the most important paintings in an encyclopedia called *Los mejores obras de arte de la historia* that my mother kept in a corner of the living room. I asked Dalia if she wanted us to go around the gallery together, and she said she did, so I was in charge of choosing which works to spend time with—although I had the feeling that Dalia was having to stifle the desire to stop before many others. But as soon as I found myself standing in front of a painting, I became tongue-tied and forgot almost everything I'd learned about it. Who the hell knows what the small dog in *The Arnolfini Portrait* is meant to represent? Let alone the mirror and the oranges. And I just couldn't remember if Velázquez's *Rokeby Venus* was revolutionary for its nudity or for the mirror. Whatever, the model is divine, commented Dalia.

I did better with the Vermeer painting of a young woman playing a virginal. I told Dalia about the domestic intimacy, the warm, oblique lighting, the woman's complicit gaze. Then I showed her the trick of the misshapen skull in Holbein's *Ambassadors*: You had to view the work from one side to see the real shape. What's the point? asked Dalia. To which I confidently ad libbed, It's an oblique symbol of death; they're hidden all over the painting. "Tacit," Dalia responded, almost to herself. I'd never actually used that word; it was lodged in some dark corner of my brain, far from spoken language. Dalia was always coming out with words that seemed amazing to me, and I'd take note and try to memorize and use them. I was embarrassed by my limited vocabulary: Too many of the books I read were in

English or were Spanish translations of books originally written in other languages. I was worried that my secret attempts at writing would sound like bad translations, like cartoon voiceovers. Dalia's Spanish, on the other hand, was florid, brimming with splendid possibilities.

I liked being able to show Dalia things in the gallery, because she knew more than me about almost everything else. Our journey through those rooms was my chance to shine, not in a competitive way—although there may have been something of that—but to interest her in my friendship, so she'd feel I was worth keeping close.

Our favorite portrait was one of a woman posing with a red squirrel on a leash. It was another Holbein, and according to the plaque, the squirrel was the lady's pet. We tried to imagine that unlikely time when squirrels, iguanas, and groundhogs were walked on leashes through the parks of Europe, and then talked about the rest of the picture: the blue background, the branches of a fig tree, a starling. We both wanted to embroider it, to find thread in that exact shade of blue and do the whole background, even if it took us years, and then embroider the black and brown starling in chain stitch and the fig leaves that looked like hands in straight stich.

We asked the gallery assistant to take our photo with the painting. And here it is, printed out and pasted into the journal of that trip to Europe. The woman in the portrait is looking directly at Dalia, as if offering to let her hold the squirrel for a moment.

We got home early and flopped onto our inflatable mattress to read for a while before sleeping. Once or twice, I laughed aloud at the eccentricities of the heroine of *We Have Always Lived in the Castle*, at the cruelty of children. Once or twice, Dalia asked me what I was laughing at. I told her, and she laughed with me.

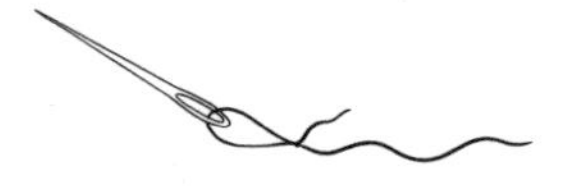

My daughter and her father are playing Scrabble. She's only eighteen months old, so she obviously doesn't know how to play, but her father insisted on buying the set so she'd become familiar with the letters. Their game consists of dumping out the tiles, piling them up, and then knocking over the piles. I'm on the other side of the living room, stitching the last letters of her name on the nursery backpack. There's something ritualistic about embroidering her name. It reminds me of the adult literacy backpack rite. During the first nighttime meeting in the assembly hall in the school in Yospí, there was an official ceremony during which the coordinators handed the ABCers each a new denim backpack, while everyone else clapped and offered words of encouragement. As I was a week late joining the campaign, they had a special ceremony for me. The backpacks already had the names of the others who'd used them on previous campaigns, and it was our responsibility to stitch our own on the one we were given. That meant all of us had to find a way to learn to embroider. The oldest backpacks were very beautiful.

At those meetings, we also welcomed the new tapancos, discussed any problems we were having in our classes, listened to reports from the various organizing committees, and voted on any important issues. I loathed them. They were held at ten at night, by which time I'd be beat. I loathed the people who somehow, from somewhere, managed to find the enthusiasm to take an active part in them, people who usually went on and on, repeating themselves, getting involved in vehement arguments about trivialities. Dalia and I never said anything; Citlali occasionally did.

We also used the assembly hall to prepare our classes during the day. There was cardstock and pens for inventing teaching materials, such as the visual-syllable game that helped students write new words: For example, starting with the word *pala*, they could then write *papa* and *papá* (if we were able to explain the accent) and then *palo*, *pelo*, *lupa*, and *Lupe*. We had to work in the morning because the majority of our classes were in the afternoon and early evening. While we were drawing, cutting out, and pasting, we listened to music on an old CD player. The idea was to take turns choosing the albums, but my choices were hardly ever played; there was a unanimous preference for Manu Chao and ska bands like Panteón Rococco and Los Fabulosos Cadillacs. I was the only one to propose Portishead or The Velvet Underground, and Iván and Citlali were the only ones to back me up—the others said it was preppy music. When all else failed, I could usually convince them to put on oldies like Violeta Parra, Mercedes Sosa, or Mono Blanco—the music of my parents' generation had found its way into my CD wallet, and I had suddenly begun to like it much more.

After a late lunch (burnt frijoles with burnt rice and tuna sandwiches), it was time for the "deliveries." The women weren't allowed to walk alone through the village; we were told it would be dangerous because of drunks—there were plenty of them, and their behavior was unpredictable. And then there were the packs of aggressive dogs trained to protect vacant lots and attack strangers, so we never went out without a stick we called a "dogwhacker" to scare them off.

My students were Rosa and José, a couple in their twenties who lived with their two small children in a house with a tin roof and a dirt floor. José worked in the nearest—it wasn't all that near—plant fabricating tepetate bricks, and Rosa sometimes went to the city to sell napkins and tablecloths. Almost all the women in the village made their own clothes—lace skirts and brightly colored blouses—and they sold white embroidery fabric decorated with running or cross-stitch. Both Rosa and José knew only the basics of reading and writing and found them extremely hard to put into practice. So the

Freire method I'd learned would be no use, and I was going to have to come up with fun reading and writing exercises to help them loosen their grip on the pencil. I was going to have to learn to teach patience.

Citlali, Dalia, and I—like almost all the other novice ABCers—arrived in that village completely illiterate in poverty. We were the daughters of parents with left-wing sympathies who, since our childhoods, had spoken to us about the unfair distribution of wealth in the world. But our comfortable lifestyles meant that we'd had minimal contact with, and almost zero real-life experience of, that injustice. Of course, we'd noticed that the women who did the domestic chores in our homes suffered severe economic disadvantage. They'd tell us or our mothers heart-rending stories of teenage pregnancies or their reasons for dropping out of school at an early age, and we really felt for them, but we had no notion of what to do about it. In our homes money was sometimes short too, but it was nothing so drastic, nothing that couldn't be solved by a scholarship to help with school fees, a cheaper apartment, or a year or two without vacations. In our friends' homes, the differences were marked by brands of clothes, subscription channels, the size and number of TVs, bathrooms, and cars. For me, friends' homes were divided between the ones that had imported Pop-Tarts and those that didn't. We saw photos of poverty in *National Geographic* and images on the annual Teletón charity show but were incapable of imagining the dimensions of inequality.

We had no conception of a house without a bathroom, had never eaten meals sitting on a dirt floor. Until then, nobody we knew or loved lived in even remotely similar conditions. And if our summer in Yospí left us with any impression, it was the pain of the attachment we began to feel for our students. The emotions we experienced made the world a smaller place, eradicated any sense of the romance of poverty, turned it into a real, urgent problem suffered by people who became dear to us, whom we came to love.

During my classes with José and Rosa, we did simple reading and writing exercises and worked through basic mathematical skills. It wasn't easy to convince them it was all worth the effort; Rosa said she was too old to learn new things and José that he had no head for reading. Even I often had difficulty in remembering just why we were doing it. Heaven knows how Freire had managed, because for me it seemed like far too short a time to learn something so complex, and if there was no follow up when the classes ended, it would all be quickly forgotten. Just how useful would what they learned be in the lives they lived? I had to remind myself of the handouts we'd read in the pre-campaign period, the story of all those Brazilian workers who, thanks to Freire, were finally able to participate in elections because the ability to read and write was a requisite for casting a vote. The coordinators would repeat over and again that even a small improvement in literacy could make a crucial difference in their lives in the contemporary world. So, we made slow progress, but progress was made.

At first, Rosa and José were very formal with me, but they gradually began to thaw and even show affection. The children invited me to play with the chickens and bugs—they used the word *gusano* the way I would *bicho*, to refer to crickets, spiders, or any kind of small animal—and there would always be a supply of vegetarian *tacos de quelites*—meat was a luxury—with freshly made tortillas.

The majority of the ABCers asked their students to teach them how to harvest maize, prepare tortillas from scratch, speak a little Hñähñu, or embroider, because they were eager to learn and carry out these traditional tasks with them, and it also reconfigured the vertical teacher-pupil hierarchy into something more horizontal. Rosa taught me to "throw" tortillas and to do running stitch, plus a few words of Hñähñu. I often repented not having insisted that my grandmother teach me the Maya spoken in the Yucatán or how to embroider *xmanikté*. She had at least showed me how to do cross-stitch; it had been a long time since I'd practiced, but my finger remembered the technique. The running stitch that Rosa called *hilván* was harder than cross-stitch: You had to keep counting the holes in the fabric and take a lot of care with the direction of the needle. But the result was beautiful; on the fabric, the cotton thread acquired the horizontal movement of water, the sheen of silk, and the figures were ancient symbols that together created a story. On the other hand, cross-stitch gave more room for creativity. Rosa and I made a traditional doll together with braids, a colorful headdress, and an embroidered flounce skirt. I wanted to do the skirt on my own, but it was turning out so awful that, doubled over with laughter, Rosa took it from me, sorted out my mistakes, and finished it herself. I also started a sampler of different stitches, outlined with running stitch, that I continued to add to afterward by copying the patterns my friends were embroidering. When I returned to the city, I even replicated the designs of the Yucatán napkins and other pieces of household linen we'd inherited from my grandmother: running stitch stars, flowers, and birds that, in some cases, were very similar to the Hñähñu ones.

One day, Rosa and José explained why they had been rather distant with me at first, why they had only barely offered to shake my hand, scarcely brushing the palm. Apparently, not long before, José had invited a stranger passing through the village to eat in their home. He'd seen the man walking along the path in the strong sunlight, sweating in his tailored suit, and, as was the custom, had offered him a taco at their table. The stranger had refused, saying he wasn't going to touch anything in that shit heap. Since then, José hadn't trusted outsiders. He was, however, very friendly with his neighbors, among them Citlali's students, Cristina and Marta, cheerful sisters who owned a grocery store. They prepared *pollo con mole* for her—she'd slip pieces to the dog when nobody was looking—and gave her cookies and cake that she passed on to me. Okay, stop now. Look at the state of me! I'd exclaim, pinching the excess fat on my belly. I'd never been heavier than at the end of that summer, and I think Citlali had never weighed less.

On the other side of the village, Dalia was teaching Fermina, a mother of three with a drunken husband who beat her. Dalia adored Fermina, said she was a brilliant woman and very upbeat, despite her situation. She helped her to get legal advice about how to sue for divorce, but then one day, after threats from her husband, Fermina refused to let Dalia into the house again. Dalia was furious but had no idea what to do; she was afraid of making things even worse for Fermina and finally admitted defeat without ever being able to say goodbye. As it was nearly the end of the campaign and she had no other students, Dalia accompanied Citlali to her classes for the remaining days.

That was when Dalia and I really started to get to know each other better. With Citlali at our side to help ease the conversation, we found that we had a lot in common. We both liked reading and were huge fans of a particular ice cream parlor in Coyoacán that served the world's best mamey sapote sorbet. Neither of us liked Nahual, a coordinator who thought he was god's gift to the human race and made Dalia and the other members of the evening dishwashing crew work in the cold schoolyard, standing around a tub covered in slugs. And in addition to all that, we were going to be in the same humanities group at school just a short time later. But we also enjoyed discovering differences: We spent hours talking about her collection of fossils or my love of music, and all that enriched our easygoing chatter with its rhythmical silences.

One day, toward the end of summer, Iván's student fell ill. Although he didn't have to, Iván still walked the three of us to our classes that afternoon (as public displays of affection were prohibited, he didn't kiss me goodbye) but said that someone else—the coordinator we called Scorpion—would come to meet us in the evening. Citlali tried to hide her excitement by pretending to look for something in her backpack: She'd fallen for Scorpion during the previous year's campaign and was still in love with him. He, however, remained theoretically faithful to the charming Diana, while flirting openly with Citlali. But then he also flirted with any other girl who happened to be around.

During my class that day, I asked José and Rosa if we could work together to write the legend of the owl they had told me about once. As a farewell present, the ABCers were going to typeset, block print, and hand sew an anthology of their students' texts. I thought the story would be ideal for the book and wanted it to be a joint effort. The legend is that owls give a warning when death is close at hand. If they hoot at night, near a house, it is because someone will soon pass away. But if they hoot in the distance, it means there will be a hailstorm. When the class was over, Rosa asked if I'd like her to wash some of my clothes the next time she went to the river. I was horribly embarrassed: Either I must stink to high heaven or she'd noticed the stains on my blouses. I shamefacedly thanked her but said there was no need.

Afterward, I went to find Citlali and Dalia at the grocery store, and the three of us waited by the side of the road for twenty minutes, half an hour, an hour, until we came to the conclusion that Scorpion had forgotten us. The last rays of sunlight were beginning to disappear from the sky. I had a flashlight: In theory, we were all meant to carry one, but the other two weren't as well prepared as me, or as paranoid. We'll get lost, said Dalia in a small voice, like a thread escaping from a closed fist. Citlali wasn't saying much either; she felt let down, her heart a hair's breadth more broken from Scorpion's forgetfulness. Dogs were barking at us, barking to each other; we walked on, arm in arm, moving slowly at Citlali's suggestion so as not to alert them. Suddenly we felt something fluttering, and as I was sure it must be bats, I ducked my head, trying to pretend they weren't there. Close by and farther off were the sounds of crickets and frogs and the twittering of nocturnal birds. I remembered the owl and told the others the legend. Hell, Mila, stop scaring us! exclaimed Citlali with a nervous giggle.

As we'd always returned in daylight before, we hadn't really taken much notice of our route, but I remembered a big medlar tree at a junction, where we had to turn. It was straight ahead from then on. There was a brief discussion about whether a certain tree we passed was the one in question. Wasn't it taller? Was there a house on the right? Or maybe next to it? We're lost, whispered Dalia nervously. Then I heard the beating of wings again and saw a shadow flying above us in the dark, and I felt frightened too. Luckily, at that moment, Citlali stepped on a medlar fruit, which she initially mistook for a piece of dog shit, and we knew we must be headed in the right direction.

When we arrived back at the school, Dalia's face was ashen; her eyes were red, but she wasn't crying. It was odd to see her so upset and frightened, because until that moment I'd experienced only her perfectly imperturbable composure. Scorpion had only just realized that he'd forgotten us and was full of apologies. He gave Dalia and me unrequited hugs—Citlali pushed him away—and offered to do our chores for the last few days of the campaign. I told him not to worry about it, said it had been an exciting adventure and I wasn't angry with him. Dalia and Citlali were seething with rage.

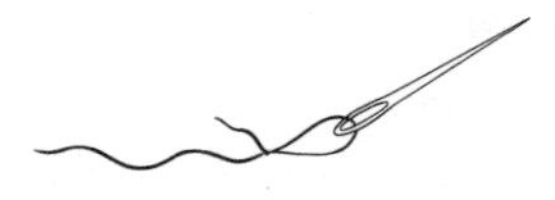

When I last saw Dalia, over two years ago, there hadn't been much chance for us to talk. She was in Mexico City for a couple of days on a last-minute trip to be with her mother, who was having minor surgery. The only time we could find to meet coincided with the only moment Andrés and I had to see another close friend, also living abroad. So the four of us went out for breakfast. I took every opportunity I could to talk to Dalia one on one, and, between interruptions, she managed to tell me that she was in love with a Puerto Rican woman but was her secondary partner: that's to say, the Puerto Rican already had a lover—her primary partner—who, by definition, received more of her time and attention, so she saw Dalia only once a week. But that suited Dalia because it meant she missed her in the intervals, and when they did meet their encounters were passionate. Plus it left her time to work. The grant she'd been awarded for her PhD wasn't enough to live on, so she'd had to take a part-time job as a proofreader for some religious publishing house—it was all there was, she said. She was also closely involved with the feminist movement at the university. They had managed to get two sexually abusive male teachers fired and were trying to improve the codes of conduct related to gender-based violence.

The arrangement with the Puerto Rican didn't seem a brilliant idea to me; I couldn't imagine why anyone would demote Dalia to a secondary role. If she wasn't going to be the only lover, she should at least be the primary one. However, she sounded happy, seemed to be enjoying a good, solid, interesting life, and I was happy for her and wanted to give her a hug but could only squeeze her forearm tightly across the tabletop. She, in turn, bent her hand around to take my wrist, and for a moment we were like that Escher lithograph of two hands drawing each other, until the waiter arrived with our food and we let go.

We didn't talk much about me. I was already pregnant by then but hadn't passed the twelve-week mark. I wanted to tell her but was afraid to do so. Dalia had always thought having children was a mistake, a trap that just led to squandering time, money, and freedom, a retrograde step in relation to the gains made by feminism. She had hundreds of very sensible arguments against the family as an institution and the conventional life I was signing up for: arguments I didn't have the resources to refute. So, in the end, I kept my secret to myself. We spoke a little about my mother and mutual friends and not at all about my work. For years, I hadn't been comfortable discussing books and my writing with Dalia, and when I did try, I felt—or she made me feel, or a mix of the two—silly: a privileged woman who was able to play at being a writer because her aunt had loaned her an apartment rent free. It was easier to talk about everyday stuff, travel, or painting; things we both loved and that weren't sensitive.

We'd discovered our shared love of painting in London, or I should say that I'd discovered Dalia's love of it, because mine was pretty apparent: My grandfather was a painter, my mother a restorer, and my father an art historian. But Dalia was more patient than me when it came to looking at works closely. She'd stand there so quietly that it seemed like she was a painting herself: portrait of a brown-skinned woman, on the border between adolescence and adulthood, dark hair with a pink streak, red sweater, hands laced behind her back, gazing at a Pre-Raphaelite painting in the Tate Britain.

We saw innumerable things on that visit to the Tate Britain before reaching the Pre-Raphaelite room, but they vanished from my mind the moment I found myself alone in front of John Everett Millais's *Ophelia*: the most beautiful dead woman in the world. I knew the story of the model by heart—how she spent whole days posing in a tub of freezing cold water and came close to suffering hypothermia. Her name was Elizabeth Siddal; she was a painter and writer and died of a broken heart after the death of her daughter. Of a broken heart and madness, just like Ophelia. I'd never liked the paintings of her megalomaniac husband, Dante

Gabriel Rossetti—those exaggeratedly voluptuous, unreal women, resembling actresses who've had too much cosmetic surgery. I hadn't liked them before I learned how Rossetti mistreated Siddal and how he buried her poems with her but then later repented, had them disinterred, and started claiming that her ghost was haunting him for having desecrated her grave. In contrast, Millais' precise hand had obsessively painted each of those leaves and flowers, had lovingly depicted the plants, the water, the girl's sodden dress. Death brimming with life.

Next to it was the portrait of Mariana, also by Millais and also based on a Shakespearian character: a woman waiting vainly in a tower for her lover's return. Mariana wears a blue dress, her hands are at her waist, and she is stretching backward in a gesture of feline somnolence.

There were very few people in the gallery that day, so I immediately sensed it when Dalia entered the room. She walked over to me and, before saying a word, did an exact imitation of Mariana's posture. We laughed aloud, but the attendant didn't see what was funny and swiveled his eyes toward us without turning his head or changing his expression. His absurd seriousness made us laugh even harder and we had to leave the room to continue voicing our hilarity in the corridor.

The map tricked us: We'd thought the Tate Britain was quite close to the Tate Modern. When we finally arrived there an hour later, exhausted, we rested for a while in the lobby, from where we could watch the swarm of people launching themselves from the third level down a gigantic slide installed by some demagogic artist.

As we had only half an hour before heading off to have dinner at my friend Iris's apartment, we decided to visit just the top floor of the gallery, where the permanent collection was housed. Although we'd thought we'd recovered our stamina, all we managed to do was to sit for a time in the Rothko room: a circular salon with dim lighting and a collection of red paintings, red on red, as if daubed in blood, like hypnotic visions from within a uterus.

I tried to explain to Dalia that my black-on-black embroidery was an attempt to do something like Rothko's red on red there and told her that he'd used black in similar paintings. I wanted to express all those thoughts, but Dalia cut the conversation short because it was already late, and we still had to buy the dessert for Iris's dinner party.

We wandered slowly through the neighborhood close to the Thames where Iris lived, tired and dying of cold. There was a cake shop with a sign for hot chocolate, and I asked Dalia to have a cup with me. It felt gorgeous to be inside, sitting under a heater, waiting for the beverage that, on arrival, looked delicious but turned out to be disgusting. The texture was like liquid plastic, and it was completely tasteless: a sort of insipid, synthetic, non-alcoholic cocktail. But even so, we both drank every drop. After a short time, our faces unfroze, and we chatted for what seemed many minutes about the chocolate, the best hot chocolates we'd ever tasted—made with water and vanilla, with green tea, cardamom, or Oreo cookies—the weirdest—with pepper and with wasabi—and the worst—also with pepper and with wasabi—among which this English beverage could definitely be included. Then we chose a beautiful white cake, decorated with lavender-colored meringue flowers. At the price they were charging, such an example of the confectioner's art should taste like ambrosia; it was the most luxurious dessert either of us had ever purchased, but it was getting so late by then that we had no other option. I insisted on paying, and Dalia insisted on chipping in something. We took a few photos of the cake in its box before leaving.

On an earlier trip to England, Iris had made friends with a member of the aristocracy and was living in a riverside property belonging to that family: an apartment the aristocratic mother of the aristocratic friend used for storage and to meet her lovers. The walls were covered in paintings she'd done herself—kitsch portraits of family members in ridiculous hats, surrounded by a plethora of dogs—and on the antique tables was a large collection of hyper-realist ceramic sculptures of phalluses, also made by the owner of the apartment.

In the entrance hall, there was an early-twentieth-century top hat. With Iris's permission, I put it on and wore it throughout the dinner. Besides ourselves, the guests were: Iris's boyfriend, Pavel, who was doing a PhD in art history; Eduardo, my Shakespeare professor;

and Douglas, a Scottish literature scholar in his seventies, in London on vacation with his wife, an English academic, who would be joining us a little later. In deference to the Scot—and also to show off—we all spoke English. All except for Dalia, who didn't say much at all and appeared to be focused on studying the people and our surroundings. The conversation progressed pleasantly until Pavel told us about a contemporary art project he'd taken part in: an installation of worn-out socks, of which he was very proud. He showed Douglas a catalog with some pictures, and the latter replied that people who did work like that lacked imagination. We all laughed a little, but when Douglas insisted that he was serious the atmosphere grew strained until his charming wife turned up to distract us. She congratulated me on my English, and I smugly boasted—read lied—that I was self-taught. But my pride was short lived, because a moment later I confused bookstore (*librería*) with library (*biblioteca*) and sank back shamefacedly in my chair. They were two words that anyone studying English literature should never confuse.

We had Thai food for dinner because the "maid" was from Thailand and cooked Iris a variety of succulent dishes each day. After a couple of glasses of wine, Iris broached the topic of my relationship with Iván and spent a long time urging the other guests to persuade me to split with him. Iris had met Iván a few times and thought he was boring and not the least good looking. And she had no reservations about telling me so. Then, for no apparent reason, she started tickling me (the top hat fell off), saying that what I needed to help me leave Iván was a good dose of rib tickling.

It was getting close to midnight, and we were thinking of leaving to catch the last train when Iris invited us to sleep over, saying there were more than enough bedrooms. So we were able to relax. Dalia was chatting with Eduardo, and I joined their conversation. Eduardo turned out to be quite engaging, even charming at times. He did imitations of the other members of the staff in my department and poked fun at the head. After a while, I went off for another slice of cake, and when I returned Dalia and Eduardo were kissing. To avoid being the third wheel, I went to sit with Iris to finish my cake, but Dalia soon joined us. What happened? I asked. She told us that when she bit Eduardo's neck, he'd let out a little squeal: Dalia hadn't liked that at all and had no intention of continuing to kiss him. I suggested she give him a second chance because he was a fun guy, and she said if I thought he was that much fun, he was all mine. I laughed but took the first opportunity to cross the room to talk to him. We were chatting about the dinner and about how hard it was to cook rice properly when he unexpectedly gave me a brief kiss on the lips. The person you really want to kiss is Dalia, I said. Well, you too, he replied and kissed me again. He was a good kisser, or at least did it differently than Iván. He led me to his bedroom. We went on kissing until I decided to bite his neck too, just out of curiosity. He uttered that small squeal Dalia had described, but it didn't bother me. What did was when he then said, Ay, you little girls, you're so aggressive! That part about "little girls" was a real passion killer, and I told him I had my period and wanted to get some sleep. Don't leave me alone like this, he said, and moved my hand to his groin. But I wasn't interested. It wasn't easy to wrench my hand from his, but I managed and heard him give a snort of disappointment as I left.

Iris assigned Dalia and me a room with a really high, four-poster bed draped with netting. When Dalia entered the room, she asked why we hadn't spent every night in that mansion. Because we thought your cousin lived like this too, I replied. The bedroom was overheated; we spent a while trying without success to discover some way to lower the settings but were too lethargic to find Iris to ask for help. Dalia wanted to know how it had been with Eduardo and I said not good—his mouth tasted of dirty puddle water.

It was so hot that we slept in our underwear. Dalia had on a lacy, lime green bra and black lycra panties. I was in white cotton. We were both lying on the same side and I could feel her warm, wine-scented breath on my neck. The bed seemed to be spinning, and I decided to turn onto my other side to see if that helped. Dalia's breath was now warming my nose. It wasn't so much a decision as an impulse: I kissed her, and she kissed me back. I put my hand to her waist, and she moved hers to my hip. We kissed slowly, gently, just a little, until

I sensed she was falling asleep. A moment later, I was asleep too, lying in the same position, embracing her. We'd kicked off the silk bedcovers.

After reading about coral bleaching—a phenomenon related to climate change that is destroying reefs—the Cornell mathematician Daina Taimina set about reproducing the complex geometry of corals in crochet. Following her model, Christine Wertheim and her sister Margaret also decided to fight for the survival of coral reefs by crocheting them. Over 8,000 people across the planet (almost all of them women) joined them in this battle using a wide variety of materials ranging from wool, cotton, and other yarns to plastics. The project seeks to weave science, art, care, intimacy, and creativity in answer to the destruction of marine ecosystems.

The idea is to get it right, my grandmother would say when I made a mistake in my stitches. I'd beg her to ignore it, but she always refused. What's the point in doing something if you don't do it well? she'd say, catching the thread with her needle and pulling stitches until she got back to the place where my error could be corrected. I used to find unpicking a bore—I hated the way the holes in the cloth were enlarged and pieces of fluff clung to their edges. My preference would have been to do what I'm doing now: sliding my scissors between the threads and the cloth and cutting them all in one go. Some of the letters on my daughter's nursery backpack look awful; I'm going to redo her whole name.

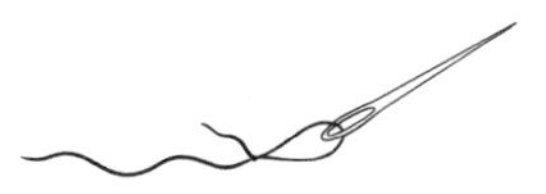

Just before the end of the literacy campaign, I had a panic attack while unpicking the stitches of my handbound books. We'd printed the anthology of the students' pieces and spent a whole day sewing them. There would be no dinner for anybody until they had completed twenty copies. I kept making mistakes: I stitched pages back to front or inserted the needle in the wrong place. I was making one error after another and getting nowhere, just sewing, unpicking, and sewing again. It was almost midnight, and I was starving. Then, when I realized that I'd messed it up yet again, I suddenly burst into a fit of laughter and wails—the two were indistinguishable. It was a completely new sensation, and I felt closer to madness than ever before in my life, in a contradictory state somewhere between anguish and exhaustion. When the coordinators heard, they took pity and gave me permission to eat.

That was a few days before our parents came to collect us in Yospí and a few days after Dalia passed me a folded note during an assembly, asking if we could talk the next morning. We sat together on a large rock on the edge of the soccer field, where there was no shade. Dalia frowned and tried to wave the sunlight from her eyes as if it were some horrible boy she was telling to get lost. I listened to her without raising my gaze from the grass around the rock, pulling up the blades as she spoke. She hated having to ask me, but would I do her a favor and not say anything to Érik about her and Bernardo. She promised that she'd come clean just as soon as we got back, but she didn't want him to hear it from someone else. She apologized for putting me in an awkward position, said the time in Yospí felt like a different life, like living in another world, and the whole thing had gotten out of hand. I told her it was no problem; I wouldn't say anything to Érik; naturally, I understood and didn't judge her. The truth is, I did judge her, but was willing to keep her secret because by then I loved her.

During those last days, we were preparing an event in which all the ABCers had to give a presentation, do some kind of performance, or whatever else occurred to them. Citlali showed us a map of the seventy hectares that composed the village that she'd embroidered with the help of her students and their children. It was spectacular, decorated all over with trees, maize fields, and animals. She rounded off her piece with a text about the geography of Yospí, its flora and fauna, and its history—how the introduction of livestock by the Spanish had led to soil erosion and the destruction of a large part of the vegetation the inhabitants had depended on for food. Goodness knows how or when, but she'd done research and interviews to expose the brutal exploitation of labor in the brickworks and the distances people now had to travel to gather the mushrooms and herbs that once grew nearby.

Dalia read a beautiful essay about the names of embroidery stitches in Hñähñu, the connection between silence and embroidery, and her theory of why in Hñähñu the names of many stitches are ways of referring to that silence. One phrase in her essay stuck in my mind: You can embroider while the children are sleeping.

From weariness and lack of imagination, my contribution was to coordinate an interpretation of the New Order song "Bizarre Love Triangle," with myself, Iván, and Citlali doing a vocal trio. Our performance included a minimal robotic dance sequence and costumes made from pillowcases and triangles of colored cardstock.

On the penultimate day, before we started packing, we all went to the closest hilltop at five in the morning to watch the sunrise. We stumbled up the slope in the dark, carrying flashlights and with unzipped sleeping bags draped over our shoulders. I was grouchy because I didn't want to go. The previous day had been long and sad: I'd had my last class with my students and was certain that I'd never see them again, that I hadn't managed to do anything except make them absurdly fond of someone who was now saying goodbye forever. The children had presented me with drawings, and Rosa had embroidered a napkin for me with a geometric cross-stitch flower, and, underneath, using the same brown thread, she'd stitched our names in freestyle: Rosa and Mila. I'd brought them the book containing their owl legend. We read it aloud one last time.

That early morning on the hilltop, hardly able to keep my eyes open, my only desire was to go home and sleep in for a whole day. We waited, resting against the trees, listening to the insects, and imagining we saw shooting stars. Iván put his arms around me, stroked my hand, and kissed me. That was the day I loved him best; it was physically painful to know we wouldn't be spending every night together in the same building anymore. We saw the sun appear between the mountains and tinge the sky, the houses, and the maize a rich red. Some people cried. I imagine I did too, because I remember that my head ached badly afterward, and I always get a headache when I've been crying.

There's an essay by Margo Glantz in which she proposes that modernity begins with the needle: "If women wrote history, the discovery of the needle and thread would be included as the beginning of the Modern Era." In the essay she explores "areas of our lives that have traditionally both liberated and constrained women." Weaving and needlework, for instance.

> The fine spinning of the Fates is an everyday, contained activity, as constrained as the embroidery within the perfect limits of a frame that stretches the fabric and allows the thread to move back and forth, tracing out hearts, flowers, and turtle doves. Writing by women always contains those cadences, that shuttling rhythm, the mythic rhythm that rises to the rooftops only to become as terrifying as the cry of the Furies when they predict Agamemnon's death at the hand of Clytemnestra, or the harsh voices Cassandra heard, yoked to Apollo's chariot, remembering the uncertain future of queens who will become household slaves, condemned to the pain of childbirth and the sweat of their brows.

Transcribing Margo's words is almost like embroidering, copying a design.

In embroidery, the designs and stitches are reproduced, shared, given as gifts, and taught. There are some still in use today that can be traced back to Ancient Egypt. Having been relegated to the category of a "handicraft," embroidery was saved from the absurd notion of originality that dominates the masculine canon of Western art. The same process can be seen in much literature written by women; we borrow the words of other women to help us express ourselves, or for the sheer pleasure of sharing, repeating, savoring them. We do this without fear or shame, delighting in those words.

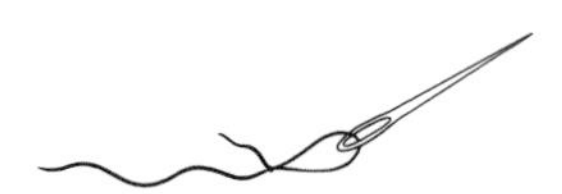

Back in Mexico City, after the campaign, the buildings seemed enormous because my eyes had become accustomed to wide, open skies. For months, the barking of dogs would make my heart beat faster. And due to some stubborn refusal of my biological clock to readjust, I continued to wake every day at the hour that had been set by the coordinators.

When classes resumed in September, Dalia was still seeing Érik. I only half kept my promise because I didn't say anything to him about the affair, but I did tell my friend Inés. I couldn't help myself; it was such a juicy piece of gossip. A few days later, Dalia broke up with Érik. I was afraid that it had been my fault, that Inés had circulated the rumor and it had reached Érik's ears. Then Érik himself told me Dalia had confessed, without asking him to forgive her. I apologized for not having told him, saying I'd thought it was Dalia's responsibility. He replied that he wasn't mad at me, but he stopped talking to me when I began to spend more time with Dalia.

A few days after the breakup, Dalia was officially dating Bernardo, who was at a different school and used to wait for her after class each afternoon, leaning against a tree on the corner. I thought it was insensitive of her to be seen with Bernardo so soon—she seemed very cruel in those days. But one morning, when we happened to be in the restroom at the same time, the sleeve of her sweater fell back slightly and I noticed that she'd cut her forearm: several horizontal wounds, still fresh and red. I pretended not to have seen anything but invited her to go for an ice cream sometime soon. She smiled and accepted.

The Dalia/Bernardo thing didn't last either. After a few weeks, she dropped him and started seeing Ernesto, a boy our own age from Andalusia whom Ignacia—one of Dalia's best friends, who hadn't gone to Yospí—had also fallen for. Among that group of friends, only Ignacia was capable of challenging Dalia's leadership: She was intelligent, very good looking, and had a *siseo*, a form of mild speech impairment that was charming and made her more human. When her friends heard about Ernesto, they came out in furious solidarity with Ignacia and expelled Dalia from the group.

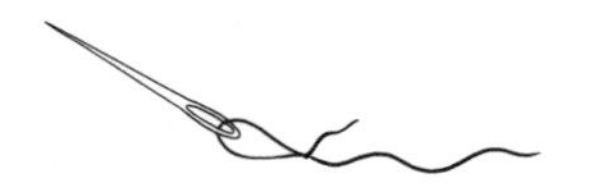

Certain artists have used their own skin as an embroidery fabric. Eliza Bennett, for example, embroidered the lines of her palm in different colors to bear witness to women's manual labor and its effects on their bodies. The title of that piece is *A Woman's Work is Never Done*. In the 1970s, the Brazilian artist Leticia Parente stitched the slogan "Made in Brazil" onto the sole of her foot as a protest against the torture practiced by the military regime.

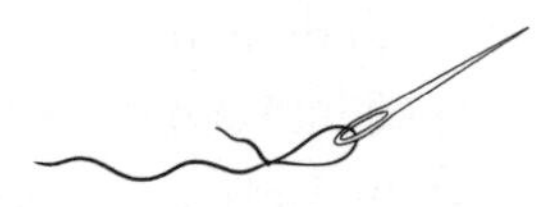

Another quote from Margo: "Cooking or other domestic activities carried out by women, such as spinning, are as historically important as the invention of bronze or the refining of iron ore: Weaving and sewing are definitive acts, much more definitive than producing an atomic bomb."

I've phoned several of Citlali's friends to invite them to the leave-taking. The idea is that they bring a passage to read aloud or an object they associate with her. Everyone asks me how it happened. My answer to them all is the same: She drowned; that's all I know.

I was always so fond of her—says our friend Alicia at the end of our call—though I never really understood her, and I guess she'll always be a mystery to me now.

While techniques for healing wounds have evolved over the centuries, a needle and thread are still commonly used. Something in the tissues, in the weaves—in their composition and the ways they recompose, reorder themselves, regenerate, reunite, and knit—may offer answers to how other wounds can be healed.

Over breakfast on our final full day in London, we talk about Citlali's latest email. She said she was feeling much better and that her aunt had deposited some money in her account. As she'd be arriving at the apartment in Paris shortly before us, she asked about where to pick up the keys.

There were two other new emails in my inbox. The first was from Iván. The subject line was: What the fuck's your problem with answering my emails? The second was from Eliseo, a student in my department, asking if I was in the city because he wanted to invite me to a concert. My heart beat faster. As I read my mail, Dalia chewed on her sandwich and explained a theory that claimed the reason English food always tastes so bad is the damp climate and the type of salt used. It wasn't so much that it actually tasted bad, but rather that the taste was less strong or the tongue wasn't able to detect the flavors. Something like that, anyway. I wasn't really listening. Dalia noticed my distraction, asked me what the trouble was, and I told her.

Eliseo was a year above me, and we were only together in one class. He was handsome, or not exactly handsome, but I thought he was because he was brilliant, could speak several languages, and had a great sense of humor, even if he was a bit full of himself. When he turned up in class late, the professor—a pain in the ass who spoke English with a fake British accent—used to say he was "too cool for school." He often cut classes, but the professor liked him anyway for being good humored and smart. I once heard Eliseo introduce himself to a girl by saying he was an author, which seemed to me dreadfully arrogant. Who introduces themselves as an author at the age of twenty? Just how much could he have published or even written? I'd felt something between curiosity and the urge to burst out laughing. Maybe he really was an author...maybe he had published a book, like those authors in the past who wrote their best work at the age of seventeen. Or maybe the simple fact of writing justified calling yourself an author, or being an author began by saying you were, pretending to be one. We used to chat sometimes in class, and one day, when we were walking to the parking lot, he offered to drop me at the metrobus station. I accepted. I liked the Iggy Pop song on his stereo. He was easy to talk to, made me laugh, and when we arrived I wanted to kiss him. I didn't, but I wanted to, and I thought he wanted to kiss me too. I gave him a peck on the cheek, and felt we were a nanosecond from a full-blown kiss on the lips when I dragged myself out of the car and ran to the station. That all happened shortly before I left for Europe, and now I had no idea what to do about his email. Even the idea of replying made me feel guilty.

But didn't Iván cheat on you? asked Dalia. Well, it depends on your definition of cheating, I responded. Anyway, I forgave him, and I'm not out for revenge; I want to be a better person than he is. Why? Dunno. You're nineteen, aren't you? Yeah. And didn't you kiss Eduardo yesterday? Yeah. So, yesterday you weren't a better person, whatever that might mean. Just answer his email. The guy sounds pretty unbearable, but do it anyway, write back, said Dalia, and she gave me an encouraging pat on the arm.

That seemed like sound advice. I continued to think it over as I brushed my teeth, then I switched off my phone and we went out.

After thirty minutes of wandering around the Victoria and Albert Museum's collection of Greek and Roman sculpture, admiring the realism and strength of its women and old men, with Dalia telling me half the story of Ovid's *Metamorphoses* and then half of his *Heroides*, we realized that all the sculptures we'd been looking at were Victorian replicas. We felt dumb. The statues suddenly appeared too polished, too bright, false. We left the room and walked for a while until we came across Tippoo's Tiger, a wooden mechanical device made in India depicting a tiger savaging a European soldier, who is lying face-up on the ground. The soldier's hand touches the tiger's face, and it almost looks as though they are lovers. The label told the story of how Tipu Sultan, the ruler of Mysore, commissioned the piece in memory of a tiger that ate the son of a powerful Englishman, and it was made in the same year as Blake wrote his poem "The Tyger." I mentioned to Dalia that I'd once dreamed I met Blake and heard him recite "The Tyger." She nodded and said drily that I'd told her that before. I was embarrassed, but the feeling passed when she started to speak with warmth and enthusiasm again and, taking my arm, wondered how it must have felt to see that mechanical tiger in action in the nineteenth century. It would have been something like seeing a Japanese robot nowadays, I replied. Dalia retorted that robots didn't impress her. So, how about watching a 3D movie or seeing a hologram? Yes, those were impressive: IMAX movies made her deliciously dizzy; she liked them as much as roller coasters. You're so right, I agreed, even though roller coasters terrify me.

I used the pretext of finding the bathroom to suggest we each go our separate ways for an hour, but the truth was that I wanted to visit the gift store to buy a few trinkets. I purchased a mirror ring, some red glass earrings, and a book about ghost cats, all of which I secreted in my backpack. Dalia went to the textile and costume collection: a crazy mix of brocades, silks, and stories, she told me on the way home. I felt silly about missing all that; I hadn't even realized that any such section existed. On the screen of her camera, she showed me the photos she'd taken of fabrics and dresses from all over the world, embroidered with hundreds of different stitches and designs. She had spectacular images of huge embroidery samplers, and we made a plan to meet up when we got back to Mexico to select and try to copy some of the designs onto our own samplers. I asked if there had been any *xmanikté*, but she hadn't noticed. Then she showed me photos of something I found deeply unsettling: a Chinese technique called *moxiu*, dating from around the seventh century, when women used to embroider representations of the Buddha in hair to demonstrate their piety. The museum's collection included images of squirrels and birds that, thanks to the hair, had the texture of real animals. They were truly beautiful but also sent a shiver down my spine. I told Dalia about the Mexican artist who'd had the bodies of his father and younger sister exhumed to make embroideries of their faces using their hair, because it was thought that the hair of the dead continued to grow after death, although science has since disproved that assumption. Dalia commented that she'd once glimpsed something in Citlali's bedroom that she now understood, or thought she did: a piece of embroidery done in hair. Maybe the hair is her mother's, I said. Who knows, could be her father's—like some kind of sympathetic magic. It's most likely Citlali's own. We're letting our imaginations run away with us. But it was weird, sort of sinister, we concluded. Dalia couldn't remember exactly what the design was, a bird or something. Citlali had never mentioned it.

We spent the early evening packing and trying to contact the concierge of the apartment we'd been lent in Paris. She was an elderly Portuguese woman who spoke very bad French but as quickly as any native. Although my French was even worse, I at least tried to talk slowly. I managed to work out that she was not happy because we'd said we'd phone her an hour before, and now she had to go out. We finally agreed that she'd leave the keys with the baker in the building next door so Citlali could collect them there.

As a farewell to London and to Iris, we had dinner with her in a small, friendly Indian restaurant with sheer blue silk curtains. She told us that Eduardo was really keen to see me again. That surprised me; I'd been sure that, if anyone, it would be Dalia. Poor Eduardo is sweet, I told her truthfully, but I'm not the least interested in him. I then asked Iris to pass on my message to avoid complications. Dalia wasn't in a good mood and hardly spoke, eating her curried vegetables and fragrant Basmati rice without raising her eyes from her plate, sighing between each mouthful: She hated the idea of leaving London. It was now her favorite city in the world, and she didn't see how Paris could be any better. No way.

That night I dreamed I was having sex with Eliseo, and he was speaking to me in a strange language that I couldn't identify. I adored it.

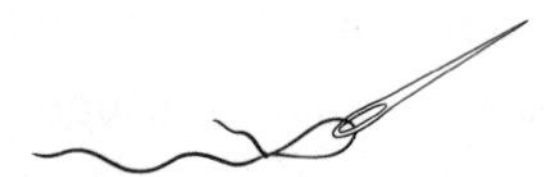

In given situations, a severed body part can be sewn back on to the live flesh of its owner, or another's body, and thus given a new lease of life.

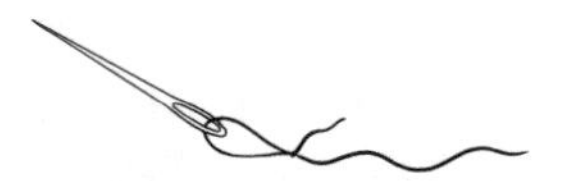

The last time I saw Citlali was at La Realidad, a café in Coyoacán we sometimes visited when we were in high school. Since then, "reality" had gone downhill, or maybe our standards had risen, but anyway, it was awful. The tea was lukewarm, our croissants still frozen in the center. And that's exactly how our conversation felt: familiar but distant, stuck ten years in our past. All too quickly, I experienced a return of the disheartening sensation that Citlali was in self-sabotage mode. Living on a boat isn't as much fun as you'd think, she said. She was tired of all the travel and felt she was being snubbed by most of the other environmentalists: some because she didn't have the appropriate academic background, and others—the radicals—because their ideas about the project and hers were poles apart.

I went off on a tangent for a moment to ask Citlali if she was eating properly—she was looking very skinny. I'm eating well, but I'm vegan now and still learning the best ways to nourish myself; that's why I'm thin, she responded. I was tempted to nag her, but even the thought of an argument wore me out, so I let it go and returned to our previous topic. I tried to convince her to be patient: She had a good job, interesting, important work; she just needed to make a little more effort to integrate into the team. But she insisted that many of her colleagues' views on conservation were maddening. They couldn't understand the impact of their actions on the communities, had no idea how to cooperate with them, and that was what most interested her, the contact with people, trying to improve their lives and the lives of every living being on the planet at the same time. I know I looked skeptical, thinking it was all just a pretext. Citlali had never been content with her life, no matter the circumstances.

She said she was going through a pessimistic phase, and all those worries were mixed up with it. She'd never believed that the organization's work could really make a difference to planet Earth, but in the past she'd thought it worth trying, in spite of everything, even if it was a lost cause. But not now. Why not? I asked. I'm not sure, she replied. Climate change is worse than they say in the media. Much worse. You can't imagine the things I've seen, the distances women have to walk to get water in some places or to find food because the plants and animals have all died off, and people end up leaving, going anywhere at all from sheer desperation. And no one cares, or not enough do, and definitely not all the businessmen, rotten with money, or the people in power— the ones who have the most responsibility for this disaster. I don't know how we're going to get out of this mess. I looked into her eyes, deeply concerned. She suggested we change the subject, but I continued to gaze at her in silence. The thing is that we're so small, she said. In comparison with the history of Earth, the time of human beings is just a blip. Like this. And she underscored her words by bringing together the tips of her thumb and index finger to indicate the size of the blip. And then we're all part of one big whole, we're made up of the same atoms, we're like a wave in the sea. Do you get it? I did, but still asked, Why all this anxiety about saving us then? Perhaps it would be better to stop thinking so much about the future and look for ways to solve whatever we can in the present. I know, I know, but sometimes it's so tiring, when not even the people who, in theory, all want the same thing can agree about how to achieve it. It just seems like we're getting nowhere, and I feel all I can do is to try to be happy, and I'm not happy in this job.

She was thinking of going to live in Oaxaca and setting up an organic produce business. Wouldn't that be beautiful? Growing tomatoes and selling mole. Wouldn't I like to come with her? I laughed. The thought of saying yes didn't even cross my mind. I was deep in a love affair with Mexico City, writing about the Bosque de Chapultepec, had a close group of friends—almost all involved in literature in one way or another—and had started dating the man who, two years later, would be the father of my child.

Don't laugh, she exclaimed, I'm serious! But then she laughed too and got a fit of hiccups. I spent a while longer trying to cheer her up: Many seemingly impossible things had been achieved thanks to the work of people like her; she should think of the children. Yeah, you go on thinking of the children, she snapped. Sorry, Mila, but I've tried hard to do something about all this. And you? Since the literacy campaign, just what have you done for a world that's falling apart around you? Write?

It's what I know how to do, I responded, offended and almost in tears. Well, yes, she replied, avoiding my eyes, but even so... She left the sentence unfinished and sat in silence, her long, straight eyelashes like the black spines of a sea urchin. Her silence was interrupted once or twice by a hiccup.

I watched her gently rubbing the sleeve of her denim shirt between her fingertips—she'd embroidered a quetzal on the left pocket, over her heart—and I thought of that old blanket she used to hold to sleep. I imagined her under the starry night skies of the African veldt, lying on a cot or in her sleeping bag, curled up with her blankie. She took it with her everywhere, on the literacy campaign, and also on our trip to Paris; it was one of the first things she unpacked.

In the end, Citlali continued to work for the environmental organization, and now I can't stop asking myself what would have happened if I'd said yes. How things would have turned out if I'd agreed to go to Oaxaca with her. Would Citlali still be alive?

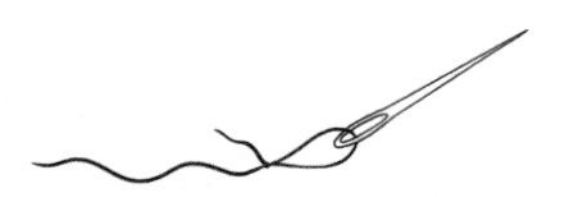

The word *pretext* derives from *praetetum*, the past participle of the Latin verb *praetexere* (*prae*: before + *textere*: weave). So a pretext can be seen as something like brocade, a piece of embroidery placed in front of the facts to justify them or make them bearable.

Dalia wanted us to travel from the airport to the apartment in Paris on the Metro rather than taking a cab, but I stood my ground, and when I offered to pay the fare, she gave way. We viewed the city like a piece of time-lapse photography, each of us looking out at the scenery on our side of the vehicle. The Paris sky was sensational, and Dalia had to admit that the city seemed to be almost as beautiful as London.

The cab rattled over the cobblestones on Rue Mouffetard, the narrow street lined with stores in the Jardin des Plantes quarter where our apartment was located. We couldn't figure out how the intercom system worked; we had no idea what the names on the metal plaques corresponded to, and, anyway, none of them belonged to the friend of my aunt who had loaned us her apartment. We pressed two or three buzzers at random, but no one answered. Then we shouted to Citlali until she appeared in a window and said she was coming down. We hugged; there were tears in her eyes, and she was grinning. I felt like crying too, but other things distracted me. I noted how thin she was, her bones seeming as brittle as dry twigs. She was wearing a coat I hadn't seen before that looked like it had come from a thrift store; her hair was cut short and dyed black. When I asked why she'd done that, she replied that it had been a sudden whim, she'd needed a radical change. The color's called black hole, she added, like my life. The way she spoke was different too. Dalia and I both laughed when she described the key as *chiquitica*. She told us that her best friend at the chateau where she'd worked was Colombian, and they'd spent so much time together that she'd caught her accent. I liked the new melody of her words: It was softer, less strident.

The Paris apartment wasn't large but was still bigger and more comfortable than our London lodgings. There was one small bedroom with a narrow bed and a living room with a full-size sofa bed. We had to work out a timetable for who got the bedroom each night. I dreaded having to sleep with Citlali because she snored loudly; I'd gotten out of the habit of using earplugs as I used to on the campaign. What's more, the sound of a single snore isn't the same as a chorus of them that, taken together, meld into a white, almost oceanic noise. I could never understand how someone as thin as Citlali could snore so loudly. She used to say it was her demons coming to life at night.

As it was already late, Dalia proposed going out for a stroll through the nearby streets to find something to eat. Citlali, who knew the city better than we did, said that it was her favorite quarter in all of Paris, and we were super lucky to be staying there. We bought fruit and bread, and I went into a cheese store for a goat's-milk Camembert. I couldn't believe such a thing existed. The variety of goat cheeses was enormous: hard, semi-soft, soft, with and without ash, with seeds or herbs.

We played rock, paper, scissors, and that night it

was Dalia's turn to sleep alone in the bedroom. Citlali and I were on the sofa bed. Citlali said that even with the lamp switched off, there was enough light coming in from the street to embroider by.

She told me about the people in the olive groves of Provence, where she'd gone after the chateau with her Colombian friend—by then almost a sister. She told me that the myth about trampling the grapes to make wine is just that, a myth, and when you're picking the grapes your whole body has to bend over in really uncomfortable, totally unglamorous positions. She spoke about two girls, one from India and the other from South Africa, whom she'd met at the chateau, and the Greek guy she'd fallen for. She showed me a photo of him—he was gorgeous. The problem was that she wasn't sure about his sexual orientation: He had a very close male friend and seemed just too beautiful to be straight. One day Citlali plucked up the courage to say *Je t'aime*. But as in French that can mean either I really like you or I love you, he'd understood it to be the former and happily replied, *Je t'aime aussi*, giving her a fraternal hug. They'd agreed to meet again in Provence, and although she was losing hope of that happening, her plan was to steal a kiss and see how he reacted.

I told her about my college courses, the new friends I'd made—oddballs, but basically good people—and about how I'd gotten used to Iván living in Ensenada, even if I did miss him at times. I'd have liked to visit him, but that summer he'd returned to his parents' home in

Mexico City. He'd been disappointed about our trip to Europe because he'd wanted to spend more time with me. Citlali figured out that I was exaggerating how good things were in my relationship and managed to disarm me with a quizzical look. I ended up telling her everything, including the Eliseo situation, and the latest inauspicious incident with Iván: He'd given me a book by Paul Auster that I'd already read. He'd seen me reading it several times while he and his family were watching American football on TV. I'd talked to him about the book and said I didn't much like it, which was a let down as I'd read other things by Auster that I'd loved. I thought he was kidding when he gave it to me, but then saw he was for real, so I pretended to be surprised and overjoyed, hugging him, thinking all the while that it was time I broke up with him. What a jackass! laughed Citlali. But if you didn't leave him over that other girl, what the hell will he have to do to make you go through with it? Maybe just something ordinary and pathetic, like that book.

After that I told her about London, what a good time we'd had, but I admitted that Dalia was driving me crazy. I warned her about the itinerary and what a voracious tourist Dalia was. I found it very hard to criticize her, feeling that she genuinely did get herself worked up about missing something important. Citlali just laughed again, yawned, and went on talking with her eyes closed. She said she didn't have any great desire to visit museums or galleries—they always ended up seeming pretentious, colonialist, middle class, and elitist. What she wanted was to walk the city with us. Plus, she had very little money, and entrance fees were so expensive. We both fell asleep while still chatting, and I was woken by her snores, a dull headache, the sound of Dalia washing dishes in the kitchen, and the sun shining through the curtains.

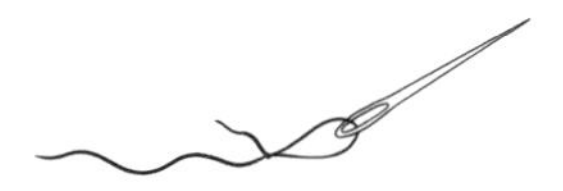

It's almost a cliché for the monsters and villains in horror movies to have stitches in some part of their body: the mouth, eyes, fresh wounds. Just the sight of those sutures is enough to make one imagine the needle passing through the flesh.

After months of toil, Victor Frankenstein succeeded in bringing to life a creature made up of the body parts of corpses. In order to obtain his materials, he killed and dismembered animals, and at night he robbed tombs and charnel houses. Frankenstein doesn't explain how he put those various pieces together, but it most likely involved serious amounts of sewing. Victor Frankenstein was, in essence, a tailor. That's how movies depict him, and his creature has stitches all over his body.

I have a recurring nightmare in which a needle so fine as to be invisible to the naked eye pierces me without my being aware of it but then remains inside me and causes me to bleed. In high school, the World History teacher told us that was how some European aristocrat was murdered just before the First World War. Everything seems to indicate that this story is untrue.

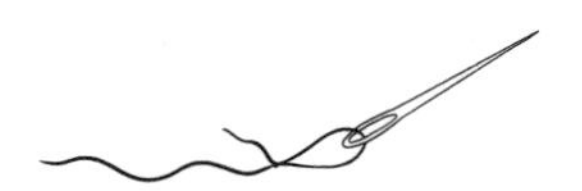

The last time the three of us were in the same space with others was at a party to celebrate Dalia's master's graduation, which coincided with a trip Citlali made to Mexico. Dalia danced the whole night long, and I spent less time than I wanted with Citlali because there were so many other people to see: college friends, friends of Dalia's who'd become mine too, friends of mine whom Dalia had adopted. Citlali was largely silent when we talked in groups, and when she did speak it was as if she were attempting to exclude others by telling some joke only I would get, talking about people the others didn't know, or referencing situations only she and I had experienced. It had been the same in high school: Citlali was lovely in one-on-one situations, but as soon as a cluster formed she became awkward and aloof.

Even our small threesome sometimes made her uncomfortable, especially in the early days, during the final year at high school, when Dalia and I began to spend more time together. She thought we were going to sideline her and let us know it through dramatic expressions and tantrums. She could be exasperating but still managed to make us feel guilty.

In that last year, we had to decide on a major. Citlali opted for biological sciences, as did most of the other girls in our year (many had scientific backgrounds). Dalia and I were the only females in the large humanities class. The friendship that had sprung up between us during the campaign grew closer when we returned to classes. The first few days we sat apart, but within a few weeks, after the second health education test, we moved to adjoining desks.

We had a couple of classes in common with Citlali, among which was health education. The teacher was one of my favorites—she had a wonderful sense of fun and knew how to hold our attention without shouting. Part of the syllabus was a concise explanation of the anatomical and neurological developments that happened during the ten or so years of puberty. She spoke with humor, but without embarrassing us, of acne, pubic hair, hormones, changes in the voice. Her lack of inhibition was contagious, and we left that class feeling more comfortable with our growing bodies.

The first test she gave us consisted of putting a condom on a cucumber. One of the students, trying to get her goat, asked for a demonstration of how to do it using the mouth. She ignored him. The second test involved giving a classmate an intramuscular injection of sterile water and then allowing ourselves to be injected in turn. Anyone who refused to participate automatically flunked. My partner, Citlali, was horrified by the exercise, as she felt injecting someone was the same as doing a piercing. For some reason, however, she didn't mind being given the injection, as long as she didn't have to watch—it wasn't the pain she was afraid of but the image of the pierced flesh. Having to inject me without averting her eyes would be torture. We tried to think up ways to do it without looking, but they all seemed dangerous, and she said she'd be able to feel it, which was almost as bad as seeing. I attempted to convince her—and myself—that it was no big deal, would be over in a flash and soon forgotten, but we both knew it wasn't going to be that simple. Citlali had shaky hands, and you only had to look at her writing to imagine what they might be capable of doing with a needle in human flesh. She'd even had medical tests done to identify the cause of her shakes and was told it was a strange but harmless condition called an essential tremor. We decided to tell the teacher about Citlali's fears, exaggerating the tremor to see if she'd take pity on us. She didn't, and told Citlali to sleep with the syringe under her pillow for a couple of weeks before the test. According to Citlali, the exercise didn't work and, what's more, caused her wake up repeatedly in the night from a bad dream in which a syringe was jabbed into her eardrum.

On the day of the test, I lay on my stomach on the aluminum table, pulled my pants down over my butt and, after a great many three-two-ones that Citlali interrupted with "Wait, give me a minute," I felt the prick. She then let go of the syringe and uttered a cry; the needle was left there just breaking the surface of my skin. The teacher intervened immediately and pulled it out. She said that attempt didn't count, told us to go outside for a breath of air, then to come back for another try. We sat in the yard on one of the blue metal benches. Citlali was sobbing, and I put one arm around her while rubbing my butt with the other.

Dalia had already been successfully given her injection by Ernesto. They were the first pair to leave the exam room and were sitting in the yard eating the lemon popsicles the school store occasionally had in stock—it was quite an event when they were on sale; the rest of the time we had to make do with the same old list we knew by heart. They came over to ask why Citlali was crying. Just think of it as a piece of embroidery, advised Dalia. Why aren't you afraid of using a needle for that? I don't know, Citlali replied. I guess because a needle can't rip fabric. But skin is just like fabric, Dalia explained; it's made up of strands too and isn't easy to tear them apart. The needle doesn't rip it, or only a little bit, and then it closes up again. It'll sew itself together again like a kind of self-darning fabric. That calmed Citlali. We sat in silence for a while until she asked if we could go back in, promising not to leave me with a needle stuck in my ass again. She kept her promise. The injection was awful because by then we were both trembling, but Citlali managed to depress the plunger, remove the needle, and apply a piece of cold cotton wool soaked in alcohol, her hand shaking throughout. The whole class gave her a round of applause.

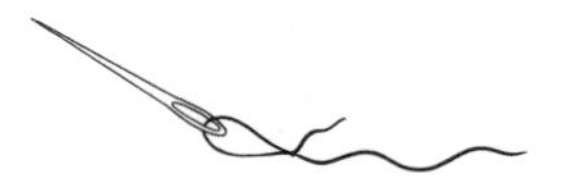

Louise Bourgeois's grandmother and mother both worked with tapestries. From them, Louise learned how to manipulate fabric as she would later do in her sculptures—usually reproductions of autobiographical events, some connected to painful experiences.

For example, the mutilated figures.

She was still a child when war broke out and her parents took her to live in the mountains, far from the frontline. A train transporting the casualties passed nearby, and Bourgeois would hear their cries. Then her father was conscripted. When he was wounded, which happened more than once, her mother would take her to visit him in the hospital. Bourgeois remembers the great number of mutilated men she saw on those visits.

The images of incomplete bodies were transformed into the rag dolls with no legs, no heads, no breasts that she later stitched.

"I've always had a fascination with the needle," Bourgeois says, "the magic power of the needle. The needle is used to repair damage. It's claim to forgiveness. It is never aggressive, it's not a pin."

But the repair is never invisible.

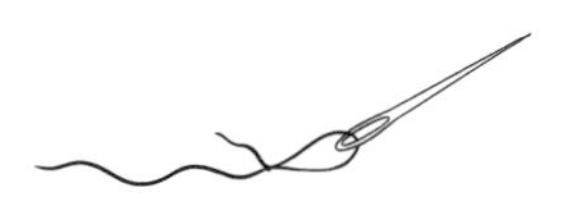

After years of writing and deleting, writing and discarding, rewriting, I managed to finish and publish a book, a collection of snippets about embroidery and the silence of women.

I sent Citlali a PDF in an email attachment because she never stayed long enough in one place to have a postal address. Within a week, she wrote back:

Mila Mía (Mimí would be a good nickname, I don't know why I didn't think of it before),

You know how bad I am at expressing myself in writing (and if anyone knows that, it must be you, because writing's your job), but I'll try: here goes. I read your essay and by the end found myself in tears. Really crying, very emotional. I was shocked, because it hadn't occurred to me that the book was going to be sad, I don't know why, perhaps because of the subject, but I thought it would be happy, upbeat, and the truth is that I really do need to smile because I've been feeling low for days, just dying to get far away again, start afresh on some mountain. I'm permanently lobster red here on the beach and I guess that's part of the problem (I've been thinking a lot about the phrase: "not even the sun warms you," 'cause that's how I feel, even if I do spend the whole damn day under that sun). Well, what I want to tell you is that I was thinking through my reaction and decided it wasn't over the top, your book deserved it. You say really sad, infuriating things about this shitty world, Mila, you jackass. Where did all that come from? I always thought you were the cheeriest of the three of us, and now it turns out that it was Dalia! Can you believe it? I remembered our novel about Adriana. You should finish it someday, you're the one who's kept on writing. I guess I'm going to have to wait a while before saying anything more, when I've managed to digest what I've read. In the meanwhile, thanks so much for your sad essay, my friend.

C

If Dalia was cheery, then Citlali and I must have been the sad ones. But I didn't believe that; Citlali made me laugh, although of course humor doesn't necessarily preclude sadness. Citlali was the one who pulled hilarious faces, did great impersonations, and told marvelous gags. I was whispered jokes, the good jokes no one ever remembered I'd told first, and that's the way my sadness was too: never spoken aloud. Dalia had a brilliantly candid sense of irony that bordered on cruelty and a deceptive sadness that more often than not turned into rage, directed at herself or others. Citlali once explained that Dalia's rages were basically optimism; she gets mad because she thinks things could have been different, that next time they will be different if we correct the mistakes. But you and I are determinists, we believe there's nothing you can do about the future, much less the past.

We were strolling together by the Seine when she spoke those words, a few steps behind Dalia, who was annoyed because we still hadn't reached Notre Dame, which Citlali had insisted wasn't far away.

But Dalia had already been in a bad mood; just as we'd been ready to leave the apartment, Citlali said she could smell gas. After hunting around for a while, we discovered that the pilot light on the stove had gone out, and it took us ages to figure out how to relight it. None of us had ever in our lives had to light the pilot on any kind of stove. Citlali said that allowances should be made for novice adults, particularly those from middle-class Mexican households, where there was always someone else to do stuff like that. At very least, they should be issued a learner's permit. Dalia finally managed to light the pilot using a match and a long strip of paper. Citlali and I were ready to celebrate her feat, but Dalia was having none of it—all she wanted was for us to stop wasting time and get moving.

I was on my last legs by the time we reached Notre Dame and had to buy a bottle of water at the first souvenir cart we came across to wash down two pills for the migraine that was throbbing inside my skull. Citlali was fresh as a daisy—she'd done a lot of walking during the past few months and was used to it; Dalia, as a climber with sporty habits, didn't seem tired either. We paused on the esplanade to view the medieval cathedral, so small that it almost seemed like we could take it in our hands to play with. Dalia had cheered up and was asking where the gargoyles were. We shielded our eyes from the sun and, with our free hands, pointed to a balcony. When we lowered our eyes, we found ourselves looking at a woman sitting on the ground, wrapped in dark clothing, panhandling with a cat on a leash beside her. The cat was resting peacefully, its eyes half closed. It's purring, said Dalia, who had three cats at home in Mexico and understood their ways. Citlali told us she'd met a man in Bordeaux who'd trained his cat to sit on his shoulder when they went out together—it was a small cat, and he had broad shoulders. Dalia approached the woman, gave her some change, and spoke a few words. The woman answered. So what's all this about having no French? I asked when she returned. I spoke to her in Spanish, replied Dalia.

We entered the cathedral. Dalia unexpectedly proclaimed that she loved the way you could almost hear tenuous echoes from medieval times bouncing off the walls. Citlali said that churches weren't really her thing: too much solemnity and too many pictures of seriously injured people, so she decided to wait for us on a bench. And there she sat, under a rose window, while Dalia and I advanced slowly but steadily through the paintings, statues, and stained glass. When we arrived at the Pietà statue and I saw the body of Jesus lying across his mother's lap, I thought Citlali must hate those images of the crucified Christ pierced by nails. It must be deeply distressing for her to come across them everywhere.

That thought was overtaken by another, almost its opposite: Excepting the part about the torture and death throes, I envied the bloodless Christ in his mother's arms. I could feel the weariness creeping up my calves and wished my mother were there to hold me in her arms. I believe I had a momentary flashback to my early childhood, of how lovely it was to be carried by her. The sensation was so vivid it actually seemed like a memory. I decided to leave Dalia with the statues and went to sit with Citlali, resting my head on her shoulder. It was one of the few physical gestures of affection she would allow: the head of someone else—a beloved someone else—on her shoulder. She asked if I knew who the people in the window across from us were. As my knowledge of church iconography was minimal, I had no idea, but the Lonely Planet guide I kept in my backpack had a paragraph that explained it: The woman was the Virgin Mary, and the rest were Old Testament characters. Citlali couldn't believe I was toting that mammoth guidebook around everywhere. Just a map would do. And anyway, Dalia had written everything in the itinerary notebook: opening times, street names, bus routes. She copied out the whole guide, said Citlali. It's no wonder you get tired, carrying such a load. At that moment, Dalia returned and suggested we go up to see the gargoyles. No, she didn't need to rest. Citlali and I sighed in resignation and followed her.

The view from the balcony was worth it, worth the stairs and the mild claustrophobia I felt in the narrow spiral. Our gazes reached out to beyond the Eiffel Tower and Montmartre. I told the others that I thought the gargoyles were cute, more beautiful than many of the dogs that were fashionable at that time. It seemed to me they were guarding not just the cathedral, but the whole city: its river, its streets, and the people on them. Dalia attempted to take photos, but the safety netting got in the way. When she told us that this church was where Antonieta Rivas Mercado committed suicide, neither Citlali nor I knew to whom she was referring. Dalia must have noticed our blank expressions and explained that she was a Mexican woman who lived in the early twentieth century: an actress, writer, and very important patron of the arts who shot herself in front of the altar of Notre Dame. I'd have preferred to throw myself from up here, remarked Citlali. I guess that's why they installed the safety net—you get the urge to jump. Do you? asked Dalia, and Citlali lowered her eyes to contemplate the abyss. Maybe not. How would you two kill yourselves? I said I'd take morphine; Dalia would climb a high peak in light clothing and die of hypothermia, looking out over the mountains: her favorite kind of landscape. That sounds good, said Citlali, but I'd be happier throwing myself off a cliff and flying for a moment.

I was beginning to find the conversation distressing and suggested we go for one of the delicious chabacano ice creams the guidebook said you could get at a nearby parlor. Dalia had never heard of chabacano ice cream and was determined to try it, but she pleaded—one of her imperative pleas—that we go to the Sainte-Chapelle first, before it closed. Wow, you really do have a thing about churches, exclaimed Citlali. I didn't say anything, because it had originally been my idea to include the Sainte-Chapelle in the itinerary, although I wasn't so keen anymore. When we left Notre Dame, Citlali looked back at the building for a moment with a mix of curiosity and revulsion. She told us that the owner of the chateau where she'd worked as a grape picker had a very beautiful miniature Buddhist temple in his garden. And did you become a Buddhist? asked Dalia. Wish I had, responded Citlali, and fell silent, as if she were thinking of all that stuff about renouncing passions and attachments. It had a lovely pond, she added, with carp and turtles.

On the way to the Sainte-Chapelle, we passed a small group of Mexican teenagers, all male, and all wearing a great deal of hair gel. They were heading for Notre Dame, and one of them said, "Hey, guys, let's just take a photo and go." The three of us laughed. Citlali said she even missed Mexican *mirreyes*. Come back with us, then, I said. The little rich brats miss you too. She smiled but didn't reply.

The Sainte-Chapelle was more stunningly beautiful and welcoming than I could have imagined. Even Citlali seemed instantly enthusiastic. It's like a Harry Potter set, she said. Dalia hadn't seen the Harry Potter movies but agreed that the chapel was spectacular. Citlali hummed the theme music of the movie as we walked beneath the blue vaulted ceiling with its gold stars, between columns, and past the rose window of the Apocalypse. Dalia took photos of everything. We should design a piece of embroidery based on that, she said, pointing to the ceiling. Metallic thread gets horribly tangled, I demurred. But we could do it, she insisted; it would just need patience. At the exit, there was a board showing the scenes from Harry Potter that had been shot in the chapel, and Citlali put on a smug expression for having guessed it.

The ice cream parlor seemed to have gone out of business; we never found it. Dalia said no way she was going to believe in the existence of chabacano ice cream until she'd tasted it.

That night I slept alone in the bedroom, and my headache disappeared.

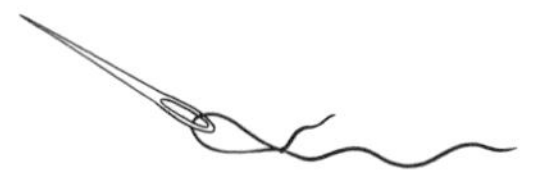

The heroine of Jean Rhys's *Wide Sargasso Sea* says that the sound of her needle going in and out of the canvas is like swearing. She's embroidering her name in cross-stitch using fire-red thread. The color of the blaze of fury with which the novel ends.

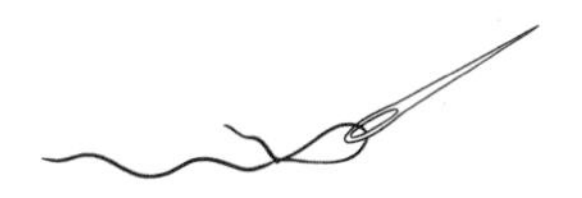

The last time the three of us were alone together was during Christmas vacation, when we met in a café near the home of Dalia's mother. I remember little about our conversation, only that we mentioned my agnostic family's tradition of celebrating the arrival of the Christmas Dragon—the ritual, invented by my mother, consisted of lighting a candle with a magnifying glass at noon and keeping the flame alive until midnight—and contrasted it with Dalia's family—atheists of Jewish descent—who didn't celebrate dragons or anything else: Christmas was just another day of the week. That was why Citlali and I usually invited her to spend Noche Buena with one of us. Although they weren't religious, Citlali's family decorated a tree, had a nativity scene, and exchanged presents. She said that by the end of the evening her tipsy aunts would be enjoying a blazing argument. The way normal people do, she pointed out; as for Dalia and me, our families were just whacky. With a bitter smile, she added, You two have more and more things in common nowadays. You have your friends, your books. I'm growing more and more like myself and less like you everyday, so it's inevitable that the equilateral triangle of our relationship becomes more isosceles. She started to trace a triangle on the polyester tablecloth with her fingertip. It finally became so elongated that it went over the edge of the table.

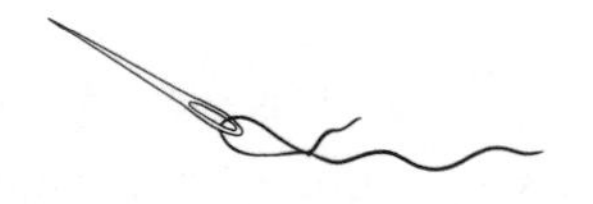

After that debacle with Citlali during the health education test, the next time I had an injection (the HPV vaccine, at my mother's insistence) I fainted. I felt silly, thought it must have been due to the thousands of times I'd read "Sleeping Beauty": my favorite fairytale when I was a child. I fainted again a few months later while having blood drawn. As a result of that, plus the death of my grandmother—whom I adored—and a few fights we had about the way I washed the dishes, my mother decided I needed therapy and sent me to an elderly Argentinian woman with dyed red hair who held her sessions in an apartment dating from the fifties. She hardly ever spoke but one day broke her Lacanian silence to unexpectedly pronounce in an Argentine oracular tone that my fear of injections—the irrational phobia that made me pass out—was a symbolic fear of penetration.

I attempted to explain that rather than being symbolic, it was a literal fear of injections, of the acute anxiety pointed objects caused or suggested to me, and anyway my fear of penetration didn't need symbols: it was literal too. I found it inconceivable that an erect penis could ever fit in the narrow space of my vagina and couldn't see how having it there could ever be pleasurable. A woman's vagina is very elastic, she told me. Remember that babies come out that way; an erect penis is nothing in comparison. Just try to relax.

I used to visit Iván at home at least two or three evenings a week. I was still very much in love with him then. I'd watched *Star Wars* to please him (I understood about half of it) and sometimes was so afraid he'd leave me that I felt like breaking things off myself, immediately, because the thought of splitting up was almost harder than the reality. I enjoyed kissing him, exploring the infinite possibilities of the kiss together. I adored his strangeness and timidity. It usually made me proud to think I was the only one to really understand him, the only one to appreciate him, even if he did occasionally drive me crazy. When we were with other people, I'd suddenly get the urge to pinch him to see if it would make him speak, to see if he'd stop hiding behind me like a child. At other times, that childlike quality made me feel incredibly tender and stirred a protective, almost maternal instinct. Iván would be going to college the next year, and just the idea of him leaving our school brought a lump to my throat.

His parents—both sociologists—were lovely, good-natured people who never made a fuss and had no problem with us disappearing to Iván's room in the evenings, with the music playing loud, necking for hours. But we still hadn't "gone all the way." Iván had a plan: When his parents visited his grandparents in Tixtla, he'd pretend to be sick so he could stay home; we'd buy condoms and do it for the very first time. He was a virgin too. At that age, I'd never heard—because no one around me used it—the word *quinto* to refer to a man who hadn't had sex, but we used virgin all the time, almost as an insult. *Virginity* signified, at the very least, an obstacle, a problem to be overcome before reaching adulthood. Losing it was the necessary rite of passage to understand the majority of movies, songs, and conversations and was also a door to an inexhaustible source of pleasure. But for women that blessed loss was also hemmed in by a series of terrifying warnings. Nobody told men it was going to be painful, that they'd bleed, ran the risk of ruining their lives by getting pregnant, that—goodness knows how—they'd be changed forever, with no hope of return. The worst men had to fear when losing their virginity was also my secret wish, and perhaps that of many other female teenage virgins: that it would all be over quickly. As the date approached, my original excitement dwindled, and the terror grew.

I was almost literally petrified, and that may be why the first time was so terribly painful. On the verge of tears, I had to ask Iván to stop. He said he'd do something to make me feel better: I thought it so funny when he licked, stroked, and tickled me that I laughed quite a lot before I came.

We tried penetration again the following day, but it was still a failure; it hurt too much. I'd heard people talking about frigid women who couldn't have vaginal orgasms and considered that to be a huge misfortune—an irreparable manufacturing fault. As far as I could see, everything seemed to indicate I was one of those women, that there was something wrong with me. Most likely because I wasn't sufficiently in touch with my body, because I was too rigid and controlling, or had some genetic abnormality.

Dalia said I had a long way to go before I could enjoy penetrative sex. She'd lost her virginity a couple of years before and was the sexual guru for our entire group of friends. Ten or fifteen times at least, she told me, after doing the math. I just had to keep trying—she assured me it was worth it.

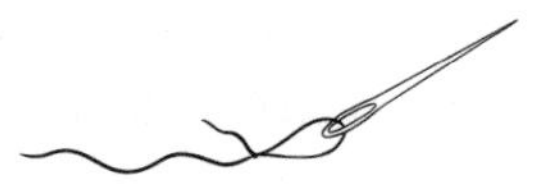

In Verapaz, Chiapas, there's a myth that long, long ago people were very cold because they had no clothes. Then the goddess Itzam came down to Earth, visited a woman in her home, and tried, without success, to teach her to weave. When she was about to give up, the goddess saw a spider and said to the woman, "Look at that spider, watch how it works and try to imitate it." And the woman learned to weave. *Huipiles* made in Cobán, Guatemala, sometimes include the symbol of a spider's web in allusion to this myth.

Nowadays it must be much less common for middle school students to pass folded pieces of paper with messages, drawings, or snatches of conversation across the classroom. I imagine they are mostly now written on concealed cell phones, with emojis, GIFs, and stickers: those new languages. In the drawer there's a notebook into which I pasted dozens of those scraps of paper with words of affection, love, or sorrow from classmates I was so fond of at that time but who are now perfect strangers—I read their names and am surprised to remember the existence of people I haven't thought about in years. "Never change," is the message that appears most frequently, exactly in the years when we were changing most. "Even if you do change, and become a male nudist named Jaime, I'll still think you're the cat's pajamas," says one from Citlali. The majority of the messages I've kept are from her, because they often have amusing drawings or stories, such as one about microscopic beings who live in the center of the earth and another about a gossipy crocodile. She was even original in terms of the materials she wrote on: concert tickets, clothing labels, or occasionally sewed onto pieces of fabric. For the latter, she used leftover yarn: embroidered messages.

I have only one from Dalia. It says, "I'm writing this message while sitting at the desk next to you. Your expression tells me you're still upset about what happened, but you managed to smile at me when you came in. I wasn't able to convince you that you're marvelous, much lovelier than those other people. I hope this message helps." I've no idea now what other people she was referring to or why I should have been feeling bad that day, but I love to imagine Dalia composing that note at the desk next to mine. Somebody should write about those teenage missives, that literary genre in danger of extinction.

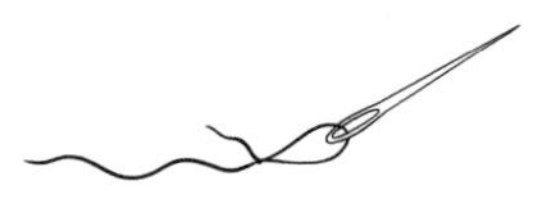

The notebooks dating from my first years at college are filled with bored doodles, quotations, and long library codes. There are other types of codes too, the ones we needed to enroll in particular classes. I'd be truly excited when the time came around to sign up for the next semester; half the professors soon turned out to be a disappointment, and I'd end up loathing some of them. But on the first day, I'd turn up to all my classes ready to be enthralled.

On that morning, in Paris, we stirred our bones early to be in an internet café by nine to sign up early for our chosen subjects before the classes filled up. Because of our good grades, Dalia and I had priority, but we were still nervous. Dalia was longing to take a Latin class with Ana María Sánchez, a very strict but brilliant professor who was a leading light in her field. I hoped to get there in time to avoid having to join Eduardo's class. After the kisses and the message I'd sent via Iris, the situation would be—to say the least—awkward. I was going to have to resign myself to taking a class in Spanish literature with The Owl, who was rumored to drool as he read erotic poetry and insisted on his students memorizing Octavio Paz's *Piedra de sol* so it could be recited during a cheese and wine picnic (for which we were supposed to provide the refreshments). Plus he made horrible remarks to the female students: "I'll give you an A," he'd told Iris, "but get out of here, you make me nervous." Ah, my darling college students, said Citlali, and pinched each of us on the cheek—a common gesture of hers, somewhere between pleasant and painful, comical and affectionate, likeable and unlikeable.

As the internet connection in the apartment was so bad, we took advantage of the visit to the café to check our email. I had a message from my cousin with contact information for the doctor who'd carried out her abortion, which I immediately forwarded to Dalia. There was another from my mother, who was extremely worried because Iván had written to her saying I wasn't answering his messages, and yet another from Iván, which said: So who are you screwing over there? Do you think I'm dumb? My guilty conscience morphed into rage and, without a moment's hesitation, I responded: Iván, there's no good way to say this, so I'll write it as it comes: I like you lots but am no longer in love with you. Sorry. I know you'll be fine. When you get over your anger, please tell your sisters and your parents how fond I am of them and how much I'm going to miss them.

I started to cry; not only had I lost a dear friend but, more importantly, his family, of whom I was extremely fond. Dalia and Citlali immediately left their computers and came to see what was wrong. When I told them, I could see from Dalia's expression that she was proud of me.

I was quickly distracted from my grief, but all too soon my head began to throb. Citlali suggested a walk to the Musée d'Orsay, and this time we didn't believe her when she said it was quite close by. But it was a perfect day for flâneuring. We took a roundabout route to include a mosque and wandered for a while among its green and blue gardens, then continued on toward the Seine. I persuaded them to stop off at Shakespeare and Company, where I strictly limited myself to the purchase of only one book. When we reached our destination, Dalia stated she didn't have time to dawdle as she wanted to see as much as possible, so we parted company and Citlali and I drifted through the rooms. I told her what I remembered from my research, imitating the explanations my mother used to give when we visited art galleries together: *Le Déjeuner sur l'herbe* had caused a scandal when first exhibited because of those naked women, sitting calmly picnicking with everything on full view; *The Angelus* was thought to have originally been a funeral painting, as there was a small coffin behind the basket around which the two peasants now stand in prayer; Degas, with his intimate and highly expressive scenes of bathers, was one of the first artists to portray the nude female body in unusual poses without sexualizing them; Courbet's *L'Origine du monde* was a watershed in erotic painting, and Lacan had once owned the canvas; Rodin was a bastard who copied Camille Claudel's work and drove her to insanity, and I didn't like his sculptures anyway.

Even though I'm embarrassed to admit it, I enjoyed playing the teacher, and Citlali seemed happy, urging me to tell her more. I don't know anything about this one, I said from time to time. Well, make something up, she retorted. And so I did: I invented theories of perspective, light, and color, stories that soon began to sound convincing, even to me. And unlike when I was with Dalia, I didn't feel nervous. Where did you learn so much? Citlali asked. You're much better than an audio guide.

We spotted Dalia in the distance, furtively taking out her phone to photograph a painting, an activity prohibited in the gallery. Even from a distance, it was clear that she was studying the works carefully. Come on, said Citlali, let's hassle her.

On our way back to the apartment, we stopped at a crepe cart belonging to a divinely enormous, bearded Viking. Dalia refused to order for herself, repeating for the umpteenth time that she didn't speak French. Don't pull my leg, we replied yet again. It's just false modesty: Your mom's a French interpreter, you're technically French, you must be able to say something. Not a word, she insisted. We still didn't believe her. I ordered the crepes, happy to chat with the blond giant, even in my poor French. I'll have a tuna one, said Dalia. But without egg; they put egg in everything here. For myself, I randomly chose something I didn't recognize, which turned out to have a sort of creamy seafood filling I wanted to eat every day for the rest of my life. Citlali forced herself to eat half a cheese crepe and then threw the rest away when she thought we weren't looking. Dalia and I glanced worriedly at each other. There were times when we wondered if she had bulimia, but had never heard her cough before flushing the toilet, which Dalia claimed was a sure sign. For some reason, we thought of her poor appetite (at the time we never used the term anorexia) as a less serious, less harsh, or at least more discreet form of attempting to vanish.

It was still quite early when we arrived back at the apartment, and we decided it would be a good idea to go to the laundromat. We packed clothes into our bags and set off down the cobbled streets, Dalia dragging her broken case, giving it a kick every so often. The seats in the laundromat were occupied by a group of teenagers who didn't appear to be doing laundry—or anything else—and who sneered at our dilapidated luggage. We didn't know how to use the machines, and there was no attendant to help us; everything was self-service. We read and reread the instructions; the machine swallowed our coins, but nothing happened. Citlali pressed the same button again and again with no luck. We were considering asking the teenagers for help, but they were by then laughing at us. When one of them remarked on how stupid we were, Citlali went up and, in furiously impeccable French, shouted that we understood everything they'd said and they were *crétins*. She stomped out of the place, attempting to bang the door behind her; unfortunately, it was on a hydraulic hinge. That made the teenagers laugh even harder. We followed Citlali, dragging our bags. At the corner store, we bought a large bar of soap to wash our essential items in the sink and dry on a radiator.

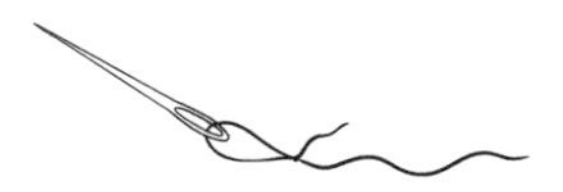

In *Earthly Paradise*, Colette watches her daughter sewing for a long time and observes that she is "silent when she sews, silent for hours on end... She is silent, and she—why not write down the word that frightens me—she is thinking."

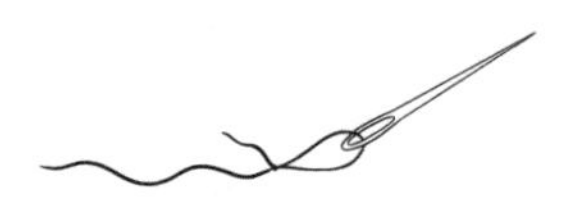

A few days before my daughter is due to start nursery school, we receive a newsletter saying that we should say goodbye to her quickly at the school door: She should walk in rather than being carried, because it would be easier, less violent, to pull her away from my legs than out of my arms. That's exactly what the notice said. So much for my dreams of her first day at nursery.

My mother says that I didn't cry the first time she took me to nursery school; in fact, after that trial day, I wanted to stay. The next morning, I asked her to take me back to the "children's place." I always liked school. At some point, I came up with the idea that my true vocation was to be a student: reading, discussing, answering the teachers' questions, becoming friends with the women and being liked by the men. To be honest, I wanted them to do more than just like me; I wanted them to adore me. Toward the end of my time at the university, I had a brief affair with one of the male professors and looked on that as the pinnacle of my academic career. At that time, Dalia and I had a theory that teaching was always a *mise-en-scène* and that seduction and eroticism were indispensable parts of the learning process. I'm not sure when—somewhere between reading rape and sexual abuse statistics and the events I myself witnessed and later reinterpreted—but I eventually came to understand how problematic, how dangerous, that theory was.

A number of our high school teachers fell for Dalia. The chemistry teacher wrote her a love letter, biology invited her to model for him in a photo session, geography asked his friend—the school psychologist—to persuade her that an older man with bushy sideburns and bad breath was a good match. It all seemed normal to us, part of the philosophy of a school that defended sexual freedom and freedom of expression to the death. Dalia had no qualms about refusing their advances nor did she feel awkward in their classes afterward. When the psychologist approached her, she burst out laughing and then walked away, leaving the woman talking to herself. When she told me about those lovestruck teachers, we'd mock them; during the final year of high school we despised almost all of them. We'd sit at the back of the room, enduring the boredom together. There were very few classes we really liked. One soporific teacher, Nacho Villar, taught us three subjects: logic, ethics, and aesthetics—a total of six hours a week. He was around sixty, and his younger wife had recently left him to move to France with her yoga teacher, taking their two children with her. Nacho had turned to drink and nihilism and spent the whole class reading us dense, obscure philosophy texts in a listless tone. Dalia and I began to bring along our needlework to help pass the time. We got the idea from a classmate who knitted socks and hats to sell and make a little extra cash. Villar didn't say anything, and we didn't either: We'd embroider through the whole class to the rhythm of Kierkegaard and Schopenhauer in the jilted Nacho Villar's laconic interpretation.

That year our roles were reversed. Citlali was enjoying her classes, liked her teachers, and was getting good grades, while Dalia and I had quite clearly had enough of it all. The only teacher we liked was Magnolia Tello, who taught an introduction to the social sciences, where we read Lévi-Strauss, Robert Darnton, and other brilliant authors. The class that sticks in my memory was when she brought in a very old, anonymous version of "Little Red Riding Hood," in which the girl seduces the wolf, throwing all her clothes on the fire and getting into bed with him. She manages to escape by pretending she needs to go to the garden to piss. At the beginning of the story, when she reaches the forest, Red Riding Hood has to decide whether to take the path of the pins or of the needles, and Magnolia explained that this was a reference to a time when girls were apprenticed to seamstresses as part of their passage into womanhood.

When our recess coincided with Citlali's, the three of us would sit on a bench in the corridor, embroidering. Iván and Ernesto—possibly Dalia's most enduring high school boyfriend—had their breaks at different times, so we were alone together. We sometimes also did the word searches in magazines we bought at

Sanborns. For a while we were addicted to them, but although that craze passed, the embroidery remained. We were always sewing, sewing together. Citlali was working on a sort of bestiary of extinct animals and plants in bright colors, and a collection of spiders and cobwebs that she called an arachniary; Dalia developed increasingly abstract designs for edgings; and I embroidered short phrases from books, song lyrics, sketches of objects, body parts, and pre-Hispanic figures on my clothes. People started to refer to us using the same adjectives (smart, affectionate, reticent, finicky, arrogant), to think of us as a single creature with two or three heads. We became inseparable, had our own way of saying things, spoke with the same lexicon and the same intonation; it was the closest I've ever been to experiencing telepathy. We were often asked if we were sisters or were told we had the same body language, were even physically alike. Citlali's jealousy dwindled, although it never quite vanished: She still occasionally got mad at us for saying something insensitive or because she felt we were excluding her. On such occasions, she'd write furious, resentful letters in which she poured out the reasons for her anger, and then others asking us to forgive her for overreacting. Dalia and I never argued, and even though we sometimes felt very annoyed with one another, we never let it show. We'd unburden ourselves to Citlali and hope the feeling would pass, and it always did pass, quickly.

If one of the three of us were absent, we'd talk

about her, analyze her inside and out, sometimes irritated, sometimes concerned. We mostly waited until we were all together to discuss anything important.

When the time came to enlist in that year's literacy campaign, both Dalia and I roundly refused. We were disillusioned with it, said we'd been able to do very little for our students. that it was a highly demanding, exhausting project with an uncertain outcome. Citlali didn't agree; she said the skills we taught were valuable and that what we'd learned ourselves was even more so, and many of the participants continued the classes in other forms, on their own or through the INEA program. She signed up for the pre-campaign, but after a few sessions dropped out. When we asked why, she was unwilling to go into detail, just said she'd changed her mind.

In addition to embroidering, Dalia and I used to read secretly in class, hiding our books between bundles of photocopies and notebooks or simply resting them on our laps, confident that our obediently downcast eyes would suffice. I was reading a lot of British authors—Jane Austen and Oscar Wilde—and Delia read everything but was particularly keen on Cortázar, Knut Hamsun, and Alejandra Pizarnik. We often discussed what we were reading, but only rarely read the same books. There was a certain pride to be found in having different literary tastes, in maintaining our own individual reading spaces, but it was also true that we were so close that what one of us read seemed to pass to the other by osmosis. We told each other everything, even the endings; if I summarized a book, Dalia commented on it and vice versa. Very occasionally we did read the same things, and when we both liked them, it was marvelous. I'd never met anyone with whom it was such a pleasure to talk literature, quote extracts, discuss authors. I don't remember anything of what Nacho Villar and the others taught us, but I still know whole passages of books I read with Dalia by heart: *The Woman Who Knows Latin*, *If on a Winter's Night a Traveler*, *To Kill a Mockingbird*, *Franny and Zooey*, *The Hour of the Star*, *A Room of One's Own*, *Morirás Lejos*. They are all stitched onto my skin.

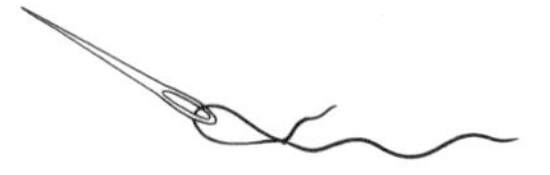

Art, says Louise Bourgeois, is the experience, or rather the re-experience, of trauma. An example of this is *The Destruction of the Father*, made from animal parts. The work was inspired by a moment in Bourgeois's childhood, when she was sitting at the table, listening to her father bragging about his achievements, and began to form a doll from bread. The doll represented her father, and once it was finished, she pulled off its legs and arms. In *The Destruction of the Father*, the carnage is transformed into a cannibalistic banquet where the children eat the father. Bourgeois says that art can exorcise fear.

I spent this past Saturday morning sewing. The invitation came from my friend Diana, who's in the habit of wheedling me into accompanying her to protests, the theater, or in this case, a collective feminist embroidery session. About twenty women sat around a long table in the renovated storeroom of a former factory. I brought along my daughter's backpack, thinking I could finish off the last letters of her name, but I'd misunderstood the idea of the event: All the participants were supposed to stitch pink crosses onto an enormous piece of cloth as a protest against the femicides in Ciudad Juárez. On the same piece of cloth, other groups of women, in other Mexican states, had previously embroidered slogans: "Stop killing us, not one more, not one less." We're supposed to decide on either "not one more" or "not one less," Diana told me; otherwise the message is confusing. We spent a couple of hours, side by side, embroidering cross-stitch crosses but made little progress, only managing to cover a quarter of the cloth. I'd forgotten just what slow work embroidery is. It's somehow like a mantra, like meditation, I said; if we keep it up, we'll attain Nirvana. My work has a very similar rhythm to embroidery, replied Diana—she's an illustrator and often creates detailed images based on embroideries. But to be honest, Diana sewed very quickly. I kept getting distracted admiring her agility: the movements of her right arm, the way she could talk to me as she sewed, maintaining eye contact, only briefly glancing back at the cloth.

Diana used the same technique to thread the needle as Citlali had during our adolescence. Citlali hated to see me wet the end of the thread on my lips to help it slip through the eye; she thought it was unhygienic, maybe even a little obscene. She was always trying to persuade me to wind the thread around the needle and then slide it along until it formed a knot at the eye, but that felt incredibly complicated and I always returned to my original technique. Dalia once gave Citlali a needle threader, which she loved, but it broke after a few days.

Citlali's embroidery designs were very different from ours. We were obsessed with mimesis: For me, it was experimenting with different fonts for writing on clothes; for Dalia it was copying increasingly sophisticated patterns. Citlali used patterns to form an outline and then, without doing any preliminary sketch on the fabric, "drew," employing different types of thread and stitches—stem, seed, chain, fly, fishbone, spider's web, four-legged knot, coral, fern, shadow, flat, backstitch, freestyle, or other techniques she invented herself and named (I remember only one, which she called "a stitch in time"). She embroidered dinosaurs, trees, penguins, bats, swings, and windows, sometimes not exactly pretty, sometimes slightly comical or naive, but always delightful. She'd show us her work in progress in a kind of secretive way, as if she were revealing something naughty; she never lost that impish expression, even when she was feeling very low.

Whenever we played hooky to go to a matinee or to the park, it was at Citlali's instigation. Particularly when we went to Viveros de Coyoacán, because she liked feeding the squirrels there, loved watching them close up, catching the moment when their claws closed in on the peanut in her hand—she'd give a nervous giggle—and admiring the speed and agility with which they crushed the shell. It's my moment of communion with nature, she'd exclaim happily, sitting on the damp ground in the shade of the Mexican cypress trees. She could name a great many of the plants we saw; her grandmother had been a skilled gardener and had taught her to identify and care for them. The balcony of her apartment in Colonia Narvarte had a small garden where she grew tomatoes and basil and cultivated exotic, self-pollinating orchids. In Paris, it made her mad not to be able to recognize the plants, and she had a notebook in which she pressed their leaves to look up the names later.

The time we played hooky from the Louvre was also at Citlali's instigation. The days had been sunny since our arrival, but this one was the best, the most luminous of all. Halfway to the museum, Citlali proposed a change of plan, saying we'd be better off going to a park or for a walk by the river. I liked the idea and backed her up: We weren't being particularly supportive of Dalia, for whom the Louvre was an absolute must. She looked at us with a forlorn expression and said we could do that if we wanted, but she hoped we wouldn't. Citlali insisted on her plan, claiming that she could summarize everything there was to see in the Louvre: king, angel, virgin, baby lamb, king, angel, virgin, mountains. All the rooms are the same. And the *Mona Lisa*? Dalia asked. Basically a virgin. And the *Winged Victory of Samothrace*? Basically an angel. Dalia asked us again to accompany her, said she was afraid of getting lost on her own and there was no way you could visit Paris without seeing *The Death of Marat*, the favorite painting of the grandfather who'd passed away before her birth. After all those deaths, there was no getting out of it.

Dalia had printed out a map of the museum, marking a detailed route through the works she wanted to see. Once again, Citlali and I drifted aimlessly down the corridors. When we spotted a large window, we made for it to gaze out on the resplendent Tuileries Garden. We stood there in silence, lost in thought, and suddenly

Citlali said, Let's go. We don't have to tell Dalia. We'll just take a walk in the park and come back in two hours. We made a dash for the exit.

Sitting on the grass near a fountain with ducks, we watched the people passing by, trying to guess which were Parisians and which tourists, and what they were all doing there on a Thursday morning: That woman works nearby and is on her lunch break; that one's playing hooky from school with her boyfriend, and they're planning to smooch in the park; that one can't afford a nanny and doesn't want to send her baby to a crèche, so she brings it here to see the ducks; that man's skipped work to decide whether to kill himself or buy a Harley-Davidson. What we couldn't work out was why the ducks were still there in winter, when, in theory, they should have migrated to a warmer climate.

A pigeon interrupted our musings. Citlali shook a few cookie crumbs from the bottom of her backpack onto her palm and knelt quietly before the bird. It approached, but then changed its mind and turned away. Come back, said Citlali. I'll put them on the ground for you!

We lay back on the grass. Citlali rested her head on her backpack; I put my head on her stomach—she didn't complain—and we stayed like that for some time without speaking, looking up at the sky and listening to the nasal twangs of the French people mingling with the sound of the water and the quacking of the ducks, who also sounded nasal and French. Then I asked

Citlali about her work—what she was going to do if she didn't get a job in any of the ski lodges or eco camps she'd applied to. Oh, here comes the inquisition, she said, poking my arm. She wasn't sure, didn't want to be cooped up in lecture theaters for four years, and wanted to work in the real world. With animals and plants, with humans, stone, and wood. There were so many things she wanted to do, and since she wanted to do them all at the same time, she didn't know where to start. And then sometimes it seemed like wanting to do all that looked a lot like not wanting to do anything. She was paralyzed. And deeply concerned about wasting time; life was too short. When I didn't answer, she complained about the cold and then asked me what I thought...but I didn't want to think. Quite suddenly, I didn't want to be having that conversation. I felt we'd had it hundreds of times before, and it was going nowhere. I suggested we return to the museum and get something to eat in the cafeteria.

We lingered over our coffees and my orange crepe and were late meeting Dalia. When we eventually found her, she was looking grouchy but didn't actually complain, and her mood soon passed. She asked what we'd seen and when Citlali replied that it had been mostly landscapes, I was unable to repress a laugh.

The next things on the itinerary were the Palais Royal and the Grand Palais, but we weren't completely certain about where they were or how far away. We crossed a few esplanades and walked between a series of different-sized columns with black and white stripes that must have been the work of some artist or other—not a very good one, declared Citlali. We passed a group of elderly men playing *pétanque*, tried unsuccessfully to work out just what the game consisted of, then came to a store selling musical boxes and went inside to admire them: There were round and square ones, some made of smooth wood and others of metal, all with their figurines or mirrors and an interminable list of available tunes. I'd buy the "Les Champs Élysées," I told them. Mine would be the "Genie in a Bottle," said Citlali. We forced Dalia to tell us her choice—in the unlikely event of her buying one. I'd have that duck, she finally decided. Just then, Citlali grasped a small wooden box too tightly and managed to break the figurine standing on top of it. We turned to check on the woman at the counter, but she was reading something in a ledger and hadn't noticed. Citlali slipped the box behind another of the same design and we walked casually out of the store.

That night, the plan was to find a restaurant close to the apartment that served fondue. We walked through the narrow streets, decorated with strings of lights, evaluating the menus on the restaurant doors, finding reasons to reject each one and continue walking, which was in fact what we really wanted to do, because in Mexico we were never able to walk alone at night. Citlali suddenly spotted a good-looking waiter at one of the sidewalk tables and suggested we go in there. While we were waiting to be brought the menu, I made a bet with the others that Dalia would be able to pick up the waiter, even with no French. But Dalia said she didn't go for pallid blonds. She did, however, like the other waiter, a slim woman with short hair and a nose piercing, but it wouldn't be easy to come on to her since she was serving tables on the other side of the room.

I attempted to ask the handsome waiter what wine he'd recommend. My French made him laugh—in a kindly way—but at least he understood what I'd said. He asked where we were from and what we'd been doing, said that his favorite part of Paris was the Latin Quarter, which he knew well because his university was there. When he left our table, Citlali and Dalia tried to persuade me to invite him to join us on our walk: They were certain he'd been flirting with me. I wasn't so sure—I was never sure until there was no denying it, until the guy was kissing me or groping my ass. I said we should leave it to fate: If the next table he came to was ours, I'd invite him along. But it wasn't, and I was too much of a coward to say anything more to him than that the fondue was delicious.

We left the restaurant, rather tipsy from the wine, took a few wrong turns, and couldn't find the way home. Dalia's cheerful mood instantly changed. I was happy—lost, half drunk, and walking through the city at night was such a luxury. I wasn't afraid of what might happen to us, not even that we might be hit by a truck because we were walking down the middle of the street;

they were mostly pedestrian zones, so that was an unlikely outcome, but even so, I imagined it and thought that if I died at that moment, I'd die happy.

Heavens knows how we got back to the apartment, but I'm certain it was Dalia—even though she was as drunk as us—who found the way.

The nightingale, says Ovid in his *Metamorphoses*, was once a young woman without a tongue. The story goes like this: Tereus had recently married Procne, who had a dearly beloved sister, Philomela. Procne asked her husband to fetch her sister and allow her to stay with them for a short time. On the journey home, Tereus fell in love with Philomela, took her to a cabin in the forest, and raped her. When Philomela threatened to denounce his crime, Tereus cut out her tongue and imprisoned her in the cabin. Philomela was unable to either call for help or to escape, but she still had her hands. She started to weave a tapestry that told her story and asked one of the guards to take it to her sister, and so she was rescued. That is when Ovid comments that grief brings great inspiration and ingenuity outwits disaster.

Sex with Iván gradually improved. It became enjoyable and tender, but I was almost always the one who made the decisions, and I sometimes felt I was using his body. Toward the end of our relationship, I'd think of other men or of nothing at all, or focus only on the pleasure, but never on him. And if the sex was often predictable, the truth was that our whole way of being together depended on a routine that was unvaried, comfortable, and ultimately depressing, like the plush bedcover under which we watched movies in the evenings. On Saturdays, I went to his place and we'd visit a video store a couple of blocks away, arguing over whose turn it was to pick: Our tastes were compatible, but we'd already rented all the good movies, and only the most cringeworthy blockbusters were left. Neither of us wanted to be responsible for choosing between those inevitable mood spoilers. Back home, we'd cuddle up on the couch in the living room in front of the television and, when the movie finished, have dinner with his family. We enjoyed being with them; his sisters were good friends, and his parents were intelligent and treated me affectionately. Iván wasn't shy when he was with his family and would entertain us with fascinating stories about entropy or the life of Galileo. He made us laugh. We never fought, and that was perhaps the worst of all: I had no reason to leave him.

A few months before Iván started college, he began to behave a little weirdly. When he was with me, he'd keep his cell phone in his pocket and was constantly glancing over his shoulder. One day, after class, from the stairs on the third floor, I saw him below, sitting with Dalia, talking secretly in a corner of the yard. They were very close together and kept looking around to ensure no one they knew was approaching. My blood ran cold. I pretended not to have seen them and left without saying goodbye.

My mother used to pick me up from school on her way home from work at three on the dot, driving the 1985 Kombi she'd inherited from my grandfather. (I hated it because it was so old and noisy.) That day, I spent the whole ride trying to figure out what Iván and Dalia had been talking about. I imagined him telling her he was in love with someone else, that he'd kissed, gone to bed with, fucked another woman: his friend Ina, perhaps, who was always laughing when she was around him, and who'd gone to a party with him the previous Friday—we hardly ever went to the same parties, preferring to see our own friends. I imagined Iván telling Dalia he'd fallen out of love with me, asking her advice about how to break things off. I wondered what would happen if he did that, and the idea saddened me because I felt calm and protected inside the relationship, even if the excitement had gone out of it. Once, everything about him had appealed to me—I'd thought his body lovely, or at very least interesting, but now his nostrils seemed too big, like incredibly deep, craggy caverns, and I hated the frayed sweater he wore every day. But above all, I hated being unable to interest him in my tastes, in the books I was reading or the new music I was listening to. There didn't seem to be anything he was truly passionate about, including physics, which he was about to study at college. Even the supposed sense of security I felt with him wasn't real because I had no trouble at all believing he was cheating on me: cheating on me with Dalia. They were friends—not close but they got along well and enjoyed each other's company. Why shouldn't they fall in love? And then Dalia had history. She'd already gotten involved with a guy her best friend was interested in. The very idea made me furious, but I realized that the thought of losing Dalia was more painful. She was capable of doing it, would go with anyone at all out of sheer boredom, because nothing and nobody ever satisfied her, and our friendship was almost certainly less important to her than it was to me.

When we arrived home, I feigned a stomachache and went straight to my room to throw myself onto the bed and sob. Then I called Citlali from our landline. She immediately told me the truth—Iván and Dalia had begged her not to say anything, but this was a case of force majeure. Dalia was helping Iván to embroider a cushion for my birthday. A whole cushion with a design of the constellations that Iván himself had devised. He'd been working on it for three months, and Dalia had been advising him on colors and finishing touches. So that was the reason for all the secrecy. I felt like a louse. I made Citlali swear she wouldn't tell them about my misunderstanding and played ignorant until my birthday came around and Iván showed up with the cushion, wrapped in purple India paper. It was the most beautiful present I'd ever received and reignited just enough tenderness to put the idea of breaking up with him on the back burner. At least for a while, until his fingers stopped hurting from all that stitching.

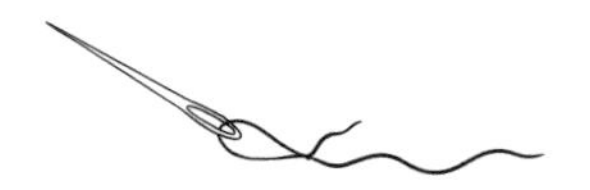

I sent Dalia a review copy of my book on embroidery. I know how busy you are, I wrote, so you don't have to read it, but your opinion would mean a lot to me. A part of me still hadn't given up on gaining her approval. I wanted to write books that Citlali would enjoy and Dalia would approve of. Books that would make Citlali laugh, would move her, and leave her at least a minimal trace of hope. As for Dalia, I wanted her to think that my books were well written and, if not spectacular or unexpected, at least devoid of obvious errors: not kitsch or silly, but sufficiently absorbing to encourage her to read them straight through. It's not that I set out with that plan, but with time I came to understand that Citlali and Dalia were the readers I was writing for, the readers I always had in mind.

Dalia replied that she'd be delighted to read the book and then didn't mention it again. I sometimes think she never opened it or, even worse, that she did and disliked it so much that she preferred to avoid the subject. Or maybe she read it but was so unimpressed that she considered it unworthy of further comment. Or she read it, liked it, but made a list of the mistakes she'd found and then had second thoughts about sending it to me. Were our literary tastes so similar, anyway?

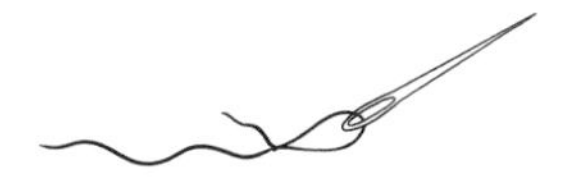

That morning Citlali had to go the embassy to renew her passport, and Dalia and I took the bus to the Père Lachaise Cemetery. The route was complicated, with several transfers, and the morning was rainy although it soon cleared up. Dalia was keen to visit Proust's tomb and told me she'd love to have her whole body tattooed with quotes from *In Search of Lost Time*. Or, at the very least, one particular phrase: "a nostalgic longing for impossible journeys through the realms of time." I said there had to be some good tattoo artists in Paris, to which Dalia replied that we wouldn't be able to bring Citlali along, because she fainted at the sight of a needle. I countered that I was the one who fainted when getting an injection. Citlali had a fear of piercings; tattoos were different. No they're not, Dalia said; you two infect each other with your phobias. And then, after a pause in which she seemed to be deciding whether or not to say more, she continued: Her dad has a piercing. Citlali's dad? Yeah, I'm not sure where. She let it slip one day. What do you mean, "let it slip"? Well, you could see she hadn't meant to say it and quickly changed the subject. We were both silent for a moment. She once told me that her father was having acupuncture. Couldn't it be that? No, it wasn't.

We'd often spoken about how much we disliked Gilberto, how horrible he was to Citlali, but I hadn't heard that story before. What do you think he's done to her? I wondered aloud. No idea, but he must have done something. Not rape her. No, something worse, more devious. What's worse than being raped? I don't know, maybe your dad not loving you. Or maybe he did rape her. There's no way we can just ask. How do you ask a question like that? I guess she'll tell us some day. I think we're seeing silkie chickens, said Dalia. What does that mean? Imagining things; he can't be such a bad person, and he must love her in his own way, just not when we're around. That's what I'm afraid of, that he *loves* her in his own way *but not when we're around*. Let's just drop the subject.

We walked several blocks up the hill, skirting the cemetery, until we came to the entrance and there we split up: Dalia headed straight for Proust's tomb, and I went to Oscar Wilde's. We could have visited the two graves together because they were quite close, but it was a kind of declaration of principles to make a choice between Proust and Wilde—in hindsight that choice seems prophetic, seems to mark the divergent paths our lives would take. I strolled along, following the route in the leaflet I'd been given at the entrance, humming a Smiths song about walking through a cemetery on a sunny day, about the people who were born, lived, and died, and how unfair dying is; about having Keats and Yeats on one side and Wilde on the other. The Paris cemetery was empty. Birds were singing in the bare branches, and there was a sound like distant footsteps. I started to hum more loudly and then to sing the parts I knew by heart. No one was listening; I could sing at the top of my voice. I stopped from time to time to admire the splendid, mossy tombs, some almost as large as houses, the statues of sobbing women and woebegone children, the occasional, usually withered flowers, and to read out the names of those dead people, their epitaphs. Out of the blue, it occurred to me to think of a cemetery as a sort of anthology, a stone book to be read while walking.

I was close to tears as I approached Wilde's tomb.

It seemed to me the worst cliché in the world to cry there, and I remembered the couple in the movie *Paris, je t'aime* who have an argument and make up there—I'd seen it on the big screen with Dalia and Citlali a year before and had liked it so much that I'd gone back twice to see it again. But despite being conscious of the cliché, I couldn't help myself; I was truly moved by the winged statue in flight and the lipstick kisses all over, the flowers, gifts, and letters. Rather than his presence or absence, more than the interred body of the author, what touched me was the love people expressed for him. And I felt that I adored him as well, that I too had a great deal to thank Wilde for. I'd just read his entire works—although not his epitaph, which I was leaving for last—but I wanted to read him better. If I'd brought a pen and paper with me, I'd have written a long, emotional letter, talking about my love of the characters he'd created, and I'd have thanked him for the laughter and complained about the anguish he'd caused me as a child, reading about his ghosts and his birds scarred by love and death—I still think that those books, classified as children's literature, are in no way written for children. I didn't use lipstick back then: I was both uninterested in makeup and incapable of applying it. Citlali didn't use it either, and Dalia only occasionally, for parties or on dates, but when she did, it looked good—her eyeliner was never wavy—because her mother was an expert and had taught her the necessary skills. Dalia tried once or twice to teach us those skills, but with no success. All I had in my backpack was a tube of clear lip balm, but I applied it and deposited a faint, oily smear on the gray stone. A phantom kiss, I thought. Before leaving the tomb, I read a message written on the stone, the most prominent of all: Viva Mexico, you bastards!

I'd agreed to meet up with Dalia an hour later at Édith Piaf's grave, which Citlali had asked us to photograph for her. I spotted Dalia again in the distance on one of the cross paths, sitting on a gravestone, her backpack on the ground between her feet, apparently reading. I came closer and realized that she was in fact embroidering: cross-stitching among the crosses. Wilde's grave had left me in a melodramatic mood and I again felt an overwhelming affection for Dalia, amazement at her beauty. I wanted to ask her to take me to Proust's tomb, to talk to me about his books, quote from them. But of course there was no available space in the itinerary, and my request would only have made her anxious.

During the bus ride back, she showed me the photos of the graves she'd visited; she'd taken selfies from above with Chopin, Jim Morrison, and Géricault. In all the shots, she was smiling. I thought that was in poor taste, that it showed a lack of respect to take selfies looking so cheerful with death all around. Quite suddenly, she seemed ugly, an ugly person, and I was also irritated by the whole business of the itinerary, her constant hurry and need to be in control. Although my anger was out of proportion to the circumstances, I blurted out: You don't get it because no one you love has ever died. You don't know what it's like; it has nothing to do with taking photos, much less grinning. I realized how ridiculous I must look, waving my thickly gloved hands in the air, and I calmed down. Dalia leaned back against the window to look directly at me. She stretched one arm over the back of the seat and gazed at me serenely, as if trying to understand me. So you have lost someone? Yes, my grandparents. Don't you remember? I was even more irritated now. Oh, sorry, I forgot, she replied. We didn't speak for the rest of the journey.

In a manual of home medicine there's a description of the basic sutures used in minor surgery that sound very similar to embroidery stitches. Their names are: running (percutaneous) suture, continuous blanket suture (over-and-over), and simple interrupted suture with a surgeon's knot (buried). For the running suture, the needle is introduced through the epidermis into the subcutaneous tissue of one edge of the wound and then pulled out through the other edge.

In Citlali's last email, she sent brief happy birthday wishes and said she was dashing off the mail because her computer had died and it wasn't easy to get another in the camp. She had no idea when she'd next be in Mexico, was trying to travel less to reduce her carbon footprint. She attached a photo of herself wearing a blue windbreaker, standing on the deck of a boat with a whale leaping from the water in the background. Below the image, she'd written in brackets, "(I found Willy and he *did* jump!)."

In my last email to Citlali, I asked how she was doing and attached photos of my daughter. I told her that I missed her. There was no reply, but that didn't worry me as I thought she must be on the boat or camping somewhere in the Amazon or the Congo, living in some harsh climate and with a non-functioning computer. I don't know if she ever got to read that email, but I decided to believe she had and didn't respond because she wanted to wait until she had time to compose a long, affectionate message, like the ones only she knew how to write. She found it terribly hard to show physical affection, but in letters she was sweeter, more generous, more expressive, and more spontaneous than me.

Through the static on the intercom, Citlali's father's voice sounded even more sinister that usual. I went up to the second floor and waited in the dark hallway for him to open the door. He uttered my name in his low, somber tone and gave me a hug. As he was tall and corpulent, that involved him bending down over me. I felt the touch of his flaccid flesh on my cheek and the bristles of his short beard. I guess the whole thing took no longer than the average hug, but it seemed to last forever. I hear you've had a baby, he drawled. One of his eyes was larger than the other, and when he smiled the difference was greater. I told him the name and age of my daughter and asked how he was doing. As you'd expect, I'm heartbroken, he responded, putting a hand on my shoulder and inviting me in with the other. There she is.

The pewter urn, engraved with a horrible band of flowers, was standing on the black piano—always in need of tuning when I visited—partially covered by a serviette embroidered with cross-stitch flowers, which Gilberto said had belonged to Citlali's grandmother. I didn't ask if he was referring to the maternal grandmother Citlali had loved so dearly or Gilberto's mother, whom she'd never known. Nor did I ask what had happened to the childhood security blanket Citlali used to take everywhere; I felt a lump in my throat, but pride or the fear that he might hug me again made me unwilling to cry in his presence. The sight of her mother's urn next to Citlali's calmed me a little. She had had few memories of her mother, most of them loosely based on stories told to her by her grandmother and aunts. Everything seemed to point to her having been a good person, a young woman who had wanted to be a singer and later decided to give music and piano classes to children. She'd known Gilberto only a short time before getting pregnant, and during the five years she had with Citlali, she'd cared for her—always patient and loving. Too patient if she was willing to put up with my father, Citlali used to say. It felt good that their ashes should be together, but not where they were. I knew that those ashes weren't Citlali herself, but I still hated the fact that they had come to rest in her father's home, from which she'd had such a hard time escaping. To which she'd never wanted to return.

Valentina told me that you're organizing a memorial for my little girl, said Gilberto, his hands clasped behind his back and his head inclined toward me—his breath smelled of Sour Jacks. Memorial service or ceremony, I don't know what the right name is. Yes, it's almost ready, I told him. I noticed how long the hairs in his ears were. Well, that's good of you. Shall we look over the details later? I nodded again. He offered me a beer. I thanked him but refused, pleading that I had to get back to my daughter. He pretended not to hear, went to the icebox, took out a beer, and placed it in my hand. We should toast her, he said. I'm just going to the bathroom and then we'll have a drink to her when I get back. I sat frozen for a moment as he went down the hallway, but just as soon as I heard the door close I put my beer on the table and followed his footsteps. The door to Citlali's bedroom stood ajar. A rectangle of greyish light from the window was reflected on the wall. The room wasn't very different from my memory of it. Over the desk was the corkboard on which she used to have photos of her mother, cousins, and the three of us, but it was now empty except for a mass of multicolored pushpins. On the bed was the cushion embroidered in running stitch that her Yospí students had given her on one of her visits. Citlali was the only one of us to return to the village after the campaign—on two consecutive years—to see her students. I searched the bed and drawers for her childhood blankie but couldn't find it.

One of the desk drawers was filled with bank documents; the next was empty. In the corner was her bookcase, the shelves holding a selection of her books: *Lord of the Flies*, *Sweet Days of Discipline*, *Mi cuaderno de bordado*, *Coraline*, *Zen in the Art of Archery*, *The God of Small Things*. Between them peeked the folded reading list. I pulled it out. Several of the books had been crossed off: *The Empty Book*, *Silent Spring*, *The Little Virtues*—the last must have been Dalia's recommendation. There was also a pile of titles from the list, still in their clear plastic wrappers, and beside them the laminated card-stock folder where she kept her embroideries and two open-topped wooden boxes that were used to hold her threads, fabrics, and scissors. The boxes were now filled with medicine bottles. A huge jar of Pepto-Bismol had leaked its pink fluid into the wood.

Gilberto must have been taking a shit because he'd been gone a long time. Vague noises were coming from the bathroom. I felt disgust, fear, and decided to leave before he could reappear. At the front door of the apartment, I called out, Have to collect my daughter! See you soon. I didn't give him time to reply before hurrying out.

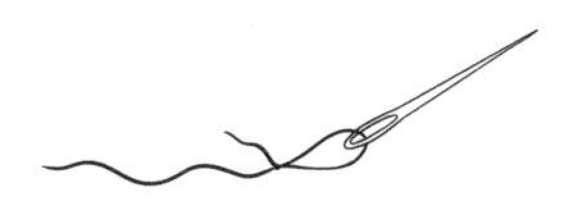

Ovid's Philomela loses her tongue. But she still has hands that are capable of saving her, has material, her loom, her needle and thread. In *Titus Andronicus*, Shakespeare bases the character of Lavinia on Philomela and, in addition to her tongue, cuts her hands off. Her uncle finds her and wonders who has "lopped and hewed...her two branches."

The poet Lexa Jiménez López, from San Juan Chamula, Chiapas, tells of how the moon taught the first women to weave when the world was still young. Afterward, she ascended into the sky, but she left behind her loom, her *huipil*, and her machete, which have been preserved. The huipiles she wore while making the world are taken out at festivals: "They were so large that now we can no longer weave them," she says.

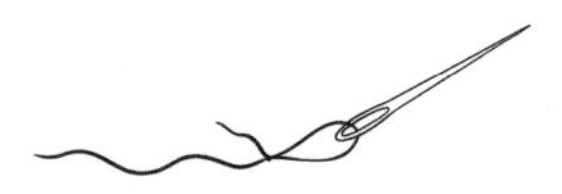

Over a year had passed since the campaign, but Citlali was still claiming to be in love with Scorpion. I asked how that was possible after such a long time, when nothing had actually happened between them, but she said that made it even worse; she idealized him, only remembering the good things: his jokes, his arms around her, his warm words, and the walks through the village at his side. She had to force herself to think of the bad stuff: that habit he had of cracking his knuckles, the revolting bandana he always wore—she was sure it stank, even though she'd never actually smelled it—the dried spittle at the corners of his mouth. Dalia and I suspected that she was just using him as a pretext, saying she was still in love because she was afraid of falling for someone else and having a real-life relationship. What about a girl? I asked her one day. I'd considered the possibility of her being a lesbian, even that she was half in love with Dalia, which might be why she was sometimes jealous of our friendship. Apparently Citlali had thought of that too, but had discounted the idea. She replied that, at least so far, she'd never felt the same about a woman. It's him or no one, she told me. I wasn't completely convinced, but maybe there was no single, clear answer; maybe she was in fact in love with Scorpion, and also a little with Dalia, because that's how things were at the time: mixed up, confusing, and intensely painful.

On weekends, the three of us used to go to parties together, or Dalia did her own thing while Citlali and I went to a concert. Dalia had sampled every available drug, her philosophy being to try them all, but only once. And as the range was so limited in those days, she eventually covered the whole gamut and mostly gave up drug use. Her current experiments were sexual: She seduced men and women, and sometimes both at the same time. She used to tell us about her sexual exploits and was such a good storyteller that I felt I already knew what it was like to do it with a woman, be in a threesome, or have a one night stand with a stranger. Inevitably, I also imagined what it would be like to be Dalia—to have sex the way Dalia did—and I fantasized about going to bed with her too.

With Iván, things continued to be uneventful. We spent increasingly less time together because he had a lot of college work. I began to enjoy the company of some of my other classmates, particularly Teo, a Chilean guy with an easy smile who had recently arrived in Mexico to finish his last year of high school. He'd become a friend of ours and soon invited us for lunch at his home—he lived close to the school. I did my best to repress my attraction for him, so that not even Citlali, with all her perspicacity and ability to read me like a book, realized. I'd stop myself the moment I began to fantasize about him, but I still got goosebumps whenever he greeted me with a kiss and his lips lingered an extra instant on my cheek, or when his fingers accidentally brushed against mine. I told myself he wasn't interested in me, but that if he ever was, I'd break up with Iván. However much I forced myself, loving Iván got harder by the day. He seemed permanently dissatisfied, disinterested in life. He wasn't enjoying his physics courses—the other students were dull as dishwater and the classes were too abstract, of no practical use, he said—and now he wanted to go to Ensenada to study oceanography. I thought it was a great idea, a beautiful profession. I bought him books on submarine journeys, deep-sea fish, and shipwrecks, and he'd accept them politely, but didn't honestly seem particularly enthusiastic. What did interest him were algae. Algae, I uttered in disillusion when he confessed this. Yes, algae: the basic, fundamental elements of aquatic ecosystems. He ended up convincing me that they were indeed fascinating organisms, but I still didn't understand how he could prefer them to whales or manta rays.

I sometimes think you're looking forward to me going to Ensenada, he said one day. Don't be silly, I replied. I told him I was excited about it because I liked the sea, although the truth was that, up until then, I hadn't known he liked it too; despite often talking about a trip to the beach during the two years we'd been together, we'd never carried through with the plan.

There were times when I found his apathy about anything but algae almost unbearable, though at other times I thought it was all perhaps normal, that my relationship with Iván might, in the end, be as passionate as any long-term, loving relationship could be. We still had the affection, the tenderness, and maybe apathy was preferable to passion as that implied some form of violence, of pain. Maybe I was undervaluing a good person due to some absurd curiosity I'd surely later regret. When all was said and done, Iván was a good man, and my grandmother, my mother, and Flannery O'Connor had already warned me that good men were the hardest to find.

Every day of that last year of high school, the three of us had lunch together. We'd leave the building at two in the afternoon and at four had a prep class for the UNAM entrance exam. In between, we'd eat at a cheap restaurant nearby or go to the fast food hall at the mall. Various friends would accompany us, and the main topic of conversation was the upcoming elections. That year, we'd be voting for the first time, and in our school the vast majority of students were divided between those on the committed left, who had absolutely no doubts about voting for López Obrador, and those on the skeptical but resigned left, who were going to vote for him because they thought he was the lesser of the various other evils. There were nonstop, heated discussions between those two bands. For my part, I liked Obrador and was certain he was the best man for the job. Dalia didn't like him but also thought he was the only real option. Citlali wasn't interested in the elections and was one of the few people still on speaking terms with the two or three students who openly supported another candidate—poor innocents who became the object of our collective, absolute scorn.

We used to return to school a little before the prep class to embroider together. We also spent many hours trying to decipher my grandmother's *xmanikté* or "forever-alive" stitch; I lent the others her huipiles to study, and sometimes Citlali would show up exclaiming that she'd figured the technique out. Then she'd try to do the stitch, but we were never convinced. We were obsessed with growing our sampler collections and now knew they were also called *dechados* in Spanish because a friend of Dalia's mother had given her a very old one that had been made by someone named Encarnación Castellanos (her name was embroidered in cross-stitch on a blue strip). Dalia's dechado dated from a time when girls in schools and convents used to practice their stitches and record them on those pieces of cloth as an aid to memory, to compare their work, and to boast of their achievements. It was a preparation for adult life. We copied many patterns from that sampler and used to imagine the child Encarnación Castellanos in the afternoons, embroidering with her friends in the garden of some school. We even invented stories about her life: that she'd been a contemporary of Sor Juana Inés de la Cruz and had been her friend, her lover, that she was the great-great grandmother of Rosario Castellanos.

The aim of our samplers ceased being to embroider the designs we practiced there on other fabrics; they became projects themselves: a collection of motifs, figures, and stitches, a set of infinite textile possibilities.

One day, Citlali and I had a conversation about vaccines, viruses, bacteria, and the multiplicity of beings that live in and make up our bodies, the illusion of the self, and the ways living organisms are all linked and mixed up together. I can't remember where I read this, said Citlali, but it's so right: "We are gardens in the wilds." I replied that I'd like to embroider that quotation, and I'd do it in cross-stitch because it would represent the idea so well: The stitches are figures, crosses that seem to be separate but are in fact a chain and a single thread. One thing.

I embroidered the quote on a bookmark in cross-stitch with an ornamental border of leaves and gave it to Citlali a few days before she left for France.

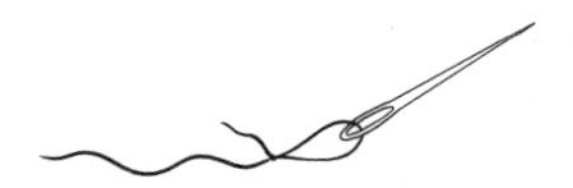

In the totalitarian regime—machista to the core, as such regimes so often are—created by Margaret Atwood in her novels *The Handmaid's Tale* and *The Testaments*, instead of being taught to read, women of the higher classes learn to embroider. Their needlework had to be purely ornamental—anything approaching writing was censured by the teachers. One of the characters in *The Testaments* enters an elite training program for women who will later carry out administrative tasks, teach, and work in the coordination and control of women in the society. And there she learns to read. A friend who is further along in the program explains that writing is like embroidery: each letter is a kind of image or a row of stitches; once you know the letters, all that's left is to learn how to stitch them together.

Toward the end, the book quotes the words of Mary Queen of Scots, shortly before she was executed: "In my end is my beginning."

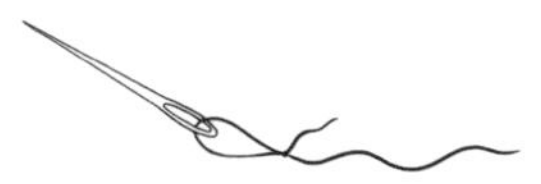

In addition to the trip to Europe and the summer in Yospí, we traveled together three times.

First, to San Miguel de Allende with my mother to celebrate my seventeenth birthday. We stayed in a hacienda with a huge swimming pool that was always too cold and ate ice cream in the plaza, near a gaunt draft horse dying of heat and thirst. For some reason I don't recall, Citlali was mad at us and didn't speak the whole day.

Second, to a house in Cuernavaca belonging to one of Citlali's aunts. I'd never seen Dalia cry so much. Milan, a drama student she adored, had just broken up with her because he discovered she'd been fucking someone else. They'd agreed to have an open relationship, but too late he realized he couldn't deal with it because he'd never be able to get the image of Dalia with another man out of his mind. Added to that, she had an allergic reaction to some plant in the garden so spent the whole weekend with red, swollen hands. We played Scrabble, and Citlali beat us. What's up with you women of letters, she exclaimed, doubled over with laughter. I was afraid Dalia was going to self-harm again and was on the alert, always going to bed after her.

Finally, to Acapulco, to a house belonging to a friend of Marie, Dalia's mother, that looked straight out to sea. Citlali found a dying seagull being picked over by grackles and carried it to the stump of a palm tree shaped like a nest. She put a towel around it and sat there for a few hours to scare off the birds so it could die in peace.

On our penultimate day in Paris, I woke determined not to speak to Dalia. I was totally pissed off. She didn't talk to me either but didn't seem mad, just aware that I was. The three of us did talk together about our plans for the day, though. We walked to the metro station and stopped en route at a pharmacy because Citlali had her period and needed tampons and something for the stomach cramps. While she was making her purchases, I pretended to be deeply interested in a nearby store window, so as not to have to talk to Dalia. There were at least thirty different types of cheese. I bought a baguette, tore off pieces during our journey, and ended by eating the whole thing.

We got off the train at Bastille and walked to Place des Vosges, where, according to our Lonely Planet, Victor Hugo had lived from 1832 to 1848. The square was possibly the most beautiful place we'd seen in Paris: green lawns with fountains and a rectangular frame of bare branches. We arrived early and, while we waited for the museum to open, sat on a bench facing a fountain. The tension between us began to bother me, so I got up to browse the neighboring stores. I bought a blue cotton skirt and stashed it in my backpack. Citlali caught up with me and asked what was going on. I told her I'd had enough of Dalia; I needed space from her for a while and that if it were up to me, I'd prefer to spend the day alone, but we had so little time left together and I didn't want to squander it. She begged me to be patient, said Dalia meant well; it was just how she was.

When we returned, the museum had opened and Dalia was at the ticket office. Citlali said that she'd wait for us outside, and I imagined she must be short of cash so I told her I'd pay, although it has to be said that she didn't seem overly enthusiastic about the visit. Because of her cramps, she didn't feel like standing to read the wall texts, and she asked me to summarize them for her. The rooms were reproductions of the different places in which Victor Hugo had lived throughout the course of his life, with a few authentic pieces of his furniture. Citlali had never read his work, and I knew only *The Hunchback of Notre Dame*. Dalia had read about five of his novels and was now examining the plaques so carefully that she was soon lagging behind us. Citlali and I continued into the next room while Dalia lingered in the Chinese Lounge, taking photos of a table with inkwells belonging to Georges Sand, Alexandre Dumas, Alphonse de Lamartine, and Hugo himself. Her hands in her pockets, Citlali moved to the window and stood looking out over the square. The sun was casting symmetrical shadows on the paths and lawns.

I walked on, wondering how I'd feel about working in a room as green as Hugo's study, or sleeping in such a red bedroom. I attempted to imagine the dreams I'd have, the books I'd write if I lived in that apartment.

I'm not sure at what point Dalia overtook us, but when Citlali spotted her leaving the museum, she followed. I hurried to catch up with them. They were ahead of me on the narrow sidewalk, walking arm in arm, laughing together about something. I had a vision of them in elementary school, saw them playing together in the yard during recess, standing very close, bending down to watch some insect. I'd almost caught up with them when I heard Citlali say she couldn't decide what she was going to do if she didn't find work: return to Mexico or go with her friend Yanina to a Greenpeace volunteer camp in Brazil. They had sent off their applications together and had been accepted. Yanina had family there who could help them find a place to stay and some undemanding job. She was really keen to get to know Brazil, to fall in love with a Brazilian man. Dalia told her to go for it, said it sounded perfect for her, and insisted that Brazilians were the loveliest people on the planet. I felt angry. How could she say that to Citlali? Couldn't she see that she was all skin and bone, flat broke, and needed the care we could only give her if she came back to Mexico? Came back to us and to her aunts, to people who could protect her. I was upset that Citlali hadn't told me about those options when I'd asked about her plans. And I was also surprised about the Greenpeace thing; until that moment I hadn't realized—possibly because of the inordinate length of time she spent in the shower each day—how important the environment was to Citlali. It was something that had always been there, but that I hadn't understood. Or perhaps it hadn't always been there; perhaps she'd changed. What did I know? That's what being nineteen was all about, changing completely in the blink of an eye.

In the Centre Pompidou, Dalia went to see the permanent collection while Citlali and I opted for a temporary exhibition of the work of Yves Klein. We loved his sense of fun, his games, his exploration of materials and color, and, of course, his unmistakable blue. We had to stop a number of times to sit on benches in the middle of the rooms because Citlali was still suffering from cramps. At some point I told her that I wouldn't want to live in a green and red apartment like Victor Hugo's but could definitely be happy in a Klein blue one, like in that song by Bowie. Citlali said she didn't remember it, so I sang her a bit. When she realized that she did in fact know it, she sang along with me.

We took the glassed-in escalators to the café, with me clutching the handrail, suffering vertigo. Someone had told Citlali that the café was the best place in Paris to watch the sunset. We'd already found a table when the menu was brought over and we had to laugh at the stratospheric prices. We ordered a bottle of mineral water apiece. The fine, elongated clouds were like the scratch marks of a cat on a blue silk curtain. Don't you want to come back to Mexico? I asked. She shook her head, her eyes fixed on the napkins. The wind lifted the shortest strands of her hair, and they looked as if they had been electrified, ready to fly from her scalp any minute. You don't want to live with your father, I said, without a question in my tone this time, and she shook her head, her eyes still on the napkins. It was the moment to ask, to finally find out what that imbecile had done to her—if he had in fact done anything more than just being an imbecile—but I swallowed my words. She looked so woeful, so pained that I thought talking things through wasn't going to help, would be too much for her. If she wasn't ready to open up, I wasn't going to make her. Citlali was silent. I put a hand on hers and felt it trembling, most likely from the condition she had, but it still saddened me. I took a few photos of the sky, and then Citlali smiled and stood next to me for a selfie of us in the twilight. You can almost see the wind in the photo I had printed and then pasted into the notebook. A gust was blowing directly onto our faces, forcing us to close our eyes.

Back in the apartment, Dalia reminded us that we had to be up at seven the next day for the early morning tour of the catacombs. I'd prefer to sleep in, said Citlali, I don't like the sound of them; I get the creeps just thinking of those skulls piled up in caves. And at that hour of the morning...it just isn't my thing. Sorry, my dear, I know you're looking forward to it.

So was I, but not so early. I'd end up with another headache from lack of sleep. I suggested we skip the tour and go to the Montmartre cemetery a little later. Dalia said, Don't be like that, you both agreed to come with me. I said maybe she could go alone, and we could meet up afterward at whatever was next on her itinerary. Dalia kept insisting, and I finally lost patience with her. I asked why she was so dependent on us, told her she had to learn to do things on her own, said it was the same with everything and that was why she could never end a relationship without having someone else lined up, and that was the reason she cheated on her partners, hurt them, and made us lie to them. She had to stop being so selfish.

In a tone that was more saddened that angry—well, a little angry by that point—Dalia insisted I was wrong; it had nothing to do with any of that. How many times did she have to tell us that she didn't speak French? Goodness knows why, but her mother had never taught her, not a phrase, not a single word. And she knew it was irrational, but the idea of being alone and lost in a city where she didn't speak the language really did frighten her. It seemed easy for us, but it wasn't for her; she felt useless and stupid, and Parisians just weren't as kind as Londoners.

I immediately felt guilty but didn't know how to express my sudden change of mood. I quietly told her that she wouldn't get lost; everyone in Paris spoke English, and they were all kind. I apologized for the things I'd said. She didn't reply, just picked up her backpack and a set of keys and left the apartment. Citlali gave me a reproachful look, but then assured me that nothing would happen; she'd be back before long.

I took a painkiller as a preventative measure and lay on the bed. And as I drowsed, I thought of how unfair I'd been, because Dalia did know how to be on her own: She read and embroidered, and those were ways of being alone. Although I then thought of the books we read and discussed together, our shared embroidery sessions, and it occurred to me that even when we did these things alone, we were together. They were our way of being alone in company.

In her book *The Subversive Stitch*, Rozsika Parker explores the place of embroidery (principally in Western culture) in the history of women and in art history, focusing on the period from the nineteenth century to the present day. She addresses the relationship between embroidery and the construction of the feminine by saying that despite the fact that embroidery creates layers of meaning, when practiced by women it is not considered an art, but an expression of their femininity, and so is immediately categorized as craftwork: a delicate, mindless, decorative activity. Parker points out the contradictions involved in embroidery; it is "a source of pleasure and power" for women but is also "indissolubly linked to their powerlessness."

She also refers to the feminist art movements of the '70s, which recovered the collective nature of embroidery. Those women shared the association of embroidery, the collective, and protest that was already apparent over a century earlier in many pieces of embroidery with anti-slavery images or suffragette slogans. A banner made by prisoners in WSPU Holloway, for example, is embroidered in purple (a symbol of dignity) with the names of eighty suffragettes who were on a hunger strike in the women's prison from 1909 to 1910. The banner was designed by Ann MacBeth, head of the needlework and embroidery department at the Glasgow School of Art, where, at the end of the nineteenth century, women were allowed to study embroidery as a recognized artistic discipline. Today, embroidered banners are frequently seen at feminist marches.

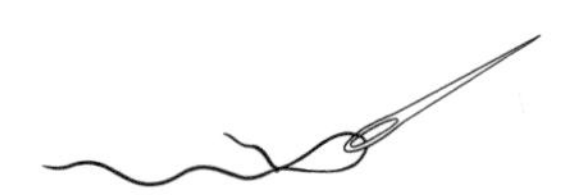

Toward the end of our time in high school, the three of us became good friends with Alicia. If we'd had more time, she might have become one of our group. We sat together in the university entrance exam classes, and she and Citlali used to exchange scraps of paper with jokes and drawings poking fun at the teacher, a woman with a shrill voice who wore T-shirts with pictures of cartoon characters.

Dalia and I were much more worried about the exam than Citlali, even though she needed a higher grade for Food Engineering than we did for Literature.

Although I never openly said it to her, Citlali's choice of major seemed to me perfect yet paradoxical. Dalia agreed, and one day told Citlali she hoped they'd teach her to eat better in her courses. If they teach me to feel hunger, that'd do the trick, replied Citlali. She said the major interested her from a social perspective, that hunger was at the root of everything.

After a great deal of prevarication, I'd applied to study English Literature, while Dalia—with no hesitation at all—was going for the Hispanic variant. A part of me wanted to study Hisp. Lit. too, and I spent a lot of time switching back and forth between those two possibilities before making a decision. The truth is that I was wavering between many other options too: mainly art history, graphic design, and biology, but with a little effort I was capable of finding something fascinating in any subject. In my indecision, my excess of enthusiasm and curiosity, I was similar to Citlali. Dalia tried to persuade me to go for History, saying she could see me studying that, could imagine me working in a museum as a curator or researcher. It upset me when she said things like that: I thought she didn't want me around, didn't want us to study such closely related majors, in the same department; that it was perhaps a form of competitiveness or the desire to avoid it; or that she might have felt that I wasn't passionate enough about books, that my passion wasn't comparable with hers.

The class trip took place just a couple of months before the end of the final semester, and our whole year and a few of our teachers were going to an all-inclusive hotel in Acapulco. Dalia was supposedly sharing with Citlali and me, but all three of us knew she'd be sleeping in another room that Ernesto had secretly booked a week or two before—she'd split up with him for a couple of months, but they were together again by then. It wasn't permitted to have separate rooms, but a cousin had been persuaded to make a booking in his own name and lend Ernesto his ID. We traveled by bus and by the time we arrived were dead from the heat, with sweat running down our backs and our ears red from the giant plastic headphones we used to listen to music—Citlali and I had been sitting together and had taken turns choosing songs. We left our bags in the room and ran to the swimming pool, which had a bar in the center serving disgusting but free cocktails called Acapultinis. The school psychologist warned us not to drink much, because either the low altitude or the oxygen on the coast made the alcohol go to your head more quickly. As if to prove her point, she was the first to get drunk and, in front of all of us, kissed Ismael—a student she was rumored to have been soft on for some time. Given this green light, Nacho Villar approached Citlali, who was alone in one corner of the pool, and tried to kiss her. Which he in fact very briefly managed to do before she reacted, pushing him away and yelling no. He said, Hey, Beanpole, I've just always thought you're so good looking, and then swam off. In another corner of the pool, I was pretending to drink while chatting with Alicia, who didn't want to get tipsy either. I saw the incident from there and then noticed that Citlali's eyelids were drooping. She looked like a child with her short hair, brightly colored one-piece swimsuit, and terribly skinny body. As far as I could tell, she was about to sink under the water. I went in search of Dalia to ask for her assistance but could tell that she was loaded too, hanging around Ernesto's neck. So I attempted to save Citlali alone and practically had to throw her over my shoulder to get her out of the pool. Alicia helped me take her back to our room, and I lay down on the bed beside her, watching television and listening to her snores.

On the third day, we were kicked out of the hotel because Nacho Villar took a piss over the balcony of his room.

When we returned from the trip, the English teacher—the same man who had introduced me to Angela Carter and who was still with us years later—decided to organize some class-trip prizes. He invented categories and went through the classrooms with a couple of students to collect our votes: Dalia and Ernesto won the "Tootsie Pop Couple" category; Citlali and Nacho Villar got "Best Kiss"; and I was "Bikini Queen," a title I found disgusting. In his class that year—a poor ripoff of the already less-than-scintillating movie *School of Rock*—each of us had to give a presentation on the band he assigned us. When it was my turn to talk about

Joy Division, he introduced me as the Bikini Queen. Outside of class, he attempted to get friendly with me, giving me novels in English and inviting me to a one-off tutorial for students hoping to study English Literature at UNAM. I detested him but behaved politely and even managed to show a little interest in his tutorial, which, inevitably, was a farce. Everyone talked about anything but the entrance requirements (an English language exam and an interview that had to be passed before taking a general knowledge test). He gave us a fumbled explanation of the dynamics and, in fact, seemed to think it his duty to scare the pants off us, saying that only twenty percent of entrants got through, and some students left the room in tears due to the difficulty of the test. After a while, I reached the end of my tether and said I had to go, and though he'd organized the meeting, it wasn't in his home, so he offered me a ride with the excuse that we lived in the same neighborhood. I couldn't think of a way to refuse. Halfway home, he told me that he'd heard a rumor was going around that he was in love with Ada, a girl with whom he did spend a lot of time during recess. But in fact, he said, blondes like Ada weren't his thing; he liked girls with pale complexions, moles, and black hair. Girls like me, that is to say. Exactly like you, he added. I started to feel uncomfortable and tried to change the subject. I told him that Ada was amazingly talented; she could draw better than anyone in the school. I kept talking so that he couldn't get a word in and located the door handle, although given that we were traveling fast down the highway, it would have been suicide to try to get out at that point. I soon began to suspect I was being melodramatic, but even so, I repented not having brought along the silver whistle my mother had given me—a pointless regret since no one outside the car could have heard it. When we arrived at my building, he leaned across and managed to put a hand on my shoulder, but one of the multiple zippers of his black jacket snagged on his seat, and that distracted his attention long enough for me to get out. I closed the car door behind me and waved goodbye. That evening, I spoke to Dalia and Citlali but was unable to make either of them understand why I was so upset. Nothing happened, right? asked Citlali. Dalia simply commented that we didn't have long left at that shitty school.

A closing ceremony had been organized for the last day of class. There was an open mic in the middle of the yard at which my classmates tearfully thanked their favorite teachers and friends. We didn't contribute, just sat together on the "cursed" bench. The story was that, a couple of years before we joined the school, a loose brick had fallen from the wall onto the head of a boy sitting on that bench and killed him. As a result, most people avoided it, but it was the only one free at that moment. Neither Dalia nor I cried. Citlali did, but it wasn't easy to figure out the exact reason for her tears, because just a few hours before, on the way to school, she'd accidentally stepped on a young sparrow and was feeling very bad about it. The chick was most likely already dead, Dalia said, but that didn't help—her favorite tennis shoes were stained with the blood and guts of the bird, and she couldn't think of anything else.

When the ceremony was over, we went to Ada's house, where we were going to have a farewell party. Citlali borrowed a pair of flip flops and threw her tennis shoes in the trash. Her feet were blue with cold, and we were talking about that when Teo came up, already a bit tipsy, and asked me to dance. He pulled me close and said that he'd always been into me, but knew I was never going to break up with Iván, so he'd finally asked Alicia to go out with him and she'd said yes. I wanted to kiss him, push him away, and cry all at the same time, but instead told him I was glad to hear the news, and so maybe he should go dance with Alicia. He continued gazing into my eyes until I bluntly suggested he get lost. And he did. I thought about going over to Citlali, but she was with Alicia at that moment, putting on songs by Gloria Trevi and Ace of Base to dance to. With tears running down my face, I finally found Dalia, and she left Ernesto for a moment to hug me.

Dalia and I passed the entrance exam with good marks. Citlali was three points short of the requirement for Food Engineering. Feeling both disappointed and relieved—she hadn't been completely certain about that major—she decided to take a gap year to travel and think through what she actually wanted to do. She found an advertisement on the internet for grape pickers in Bordeaux and applied immediately.

That summer, I was supposed to go on a trip to Colombia with Iván and his family, although it nearly didn't happen. A few days before our departure, a friend told me on chat that he'd seen Iván kissing Ina, his best female friend, at a party some months before. I'd always thought that Ina tended to flirt with him but had told myself it was nothing more than silly jealousy on my part, a lack of trust in men resulting from my father's behavior.

My initial reaction was that there must be some mistake, and I calmly asked Iván about the episode over the phone. He didn't even deny it, just cried. He said all the usual stuff: He'd been drunk, it hadn't meant anything, he loved me, I should give him another chance, he couldn't live without me, it had just been a few kisses. More than one kiss? I asked, still a little incredulous but beginning to get quite angry. Everything about the situation, particularly his sniveling tone, made me sick. He went on talking, begging me to go to Colombia with him, saying it would be like making a fresh start.

I hung up and spent the whole of the next day thinking the matter through, leaving his texts and calls unanswered. It seemed indisputable that I had to break up with him, but a part of me still resisted. I wanted to go to Colombia, and I finally came to the conclusion that I could make up my mind during the trip. Dalia and Citlali thought that was a bad idea, almost begged me to leave him once and for all. I'm speaking from experience, said Dalia. If he's done it once, he'll do it again. But I was determined to use the trip to make a decision. On our second day in Cartagena, Iván got a stomach bug and didn't leave the hotel again for the rest of the vacation. His sisters, parents, and I were, on the other hand, enjoying ourselves, laughing as we walked through the colonial streets and swam from paradisiacal beaches. It was as if Iván had never come with us, so I decided to give him a month longer. The mere idea of all the steps involved in breaking up with him—sitting down to explain my reasons, listening to him cry and make promises—irritated me. The thought of saying goodbye to his family was heartbreaking. Plus, after the vacation, Iván was more charming than ever: He bought me presents and sent long love letters—on paper, not by email or text—decorated with drawings of animals and plants.

While I was in Colombia, Dalia read *War and Peace*, and Citlali spent two weeks with her aunt visiting Japan and China. When the three of us were together again, we started meeting up at Dalia's to try to decipher the instructions in the Japanese book on embroidery that Citlali had bought—the whale I attempted to copy from it was a disaster, more like a blue pewter pot than a marine mammal. She told us the marvelous story of Nushu: Chinese women were traditionally not taught to read or write, so they had created a secret language to communicate among themselves. It was an oral and written language, which they embroidered, wove, or painted onto fans and other objects. She spoke of a bronze nineteenth-century coin, the oldest known example of Nushu writing, which read, "All the women in the world are members of the same family."

Shortly after her return, Citlali tripped on the stairs of Tacubaya metro station and broke her right wrist. During the time she was in a cast, she embroidered with her left hand: chaotic stitches that formed very beautiful abstract designs.

One afternoon around that time, Dalia asked us to come over, and we found her crying in her room. We sat on the bed next to her, Citlali constantly scratching under the cast with a pencil. Dalia told us that she and Alicia had gone to a party given by one of Alicia's cousins, whom she'd thought good looking. The party was at his house, and she'd danced with him until everyone else left. They'd chatted for a long time, then started necking, and then suddenly she'd stopped liking him: His fingers fumbled, becoming less gentle as he caressed her, and his kisses grew more perfunctory. When she said she wanted to leave, he got mad. He called her a cocktease and brutally forced himself on her. Her wrists and arms were covered in bruises.

We considered reporting the crime, but Dalia wasn't interested. She told us she'd gotten ahold of his email address and had written to say she had evidence and if he ever came near her again, she'd go to the police. Just in case, we took photos of the marks on her arms. She made us promise to let the matter drop and not to say anything to Alicia or her mother. I felt like going over and kneecapping him. I spent awhile thinking about who we could round up to help do something like that, but Iván was too whispy, as were most of my male friends. Then I remembered the Shit Band; a friend had once said she'd heard of a group of people that, for a modest fee, would smear a person's front door with excrement in the night, but Dalia didn't want that either. My lust for revenge was frustrated.

For the rest of the summer, Dalia stayed home and read. She seemed fine, unruffled. I brought her desserts whenever I could and rented movies to watch together while we embroidered. She refused to talk about what had happened.

During that time, I told myself I was just waiting for the right moment to end things with Iván, but when the perfect moment arrived, when he was finally going away to college in Ensenada, he begged me not to leave him, said he'd prefer to stay in the city, drop out of school; he claimed he'd kill himself if he lost me. I was flattered to feel so needed, to be so important in someone's life, but was also afraid he might actually commit suicide since he'd never said anything quite like that before. What's more, he promised he'd come to visit me every other weekend, and that sounded to me like an ideal relationship, with plenty of time to read, sew, write, and be with my female friends. So, in the end, I didn't break off the relationship.

Iván went to Ensenada, Dalia and I started studying at UNAM, and shortly after that Citlali went to France. Her aunt Valentina, Dalia, and I saw her off at the airport. Gilberto didn't come with us. When we said goodbye I was on the verge of tears, not knowing when I'd see her again. All I was capable of uttering was, Take good care of yourself. Dalia whispered something more into her ear that I didn't catch. She stroked Citlali's hair, and Citlali didn't protest.

A few days after Citlali's departure, Dalia went to bed with Scorpion at a party. I didn't go to bed with anyone, she protested; we fucked standing up, against the sink in the bathroom. She asked me not to say anything to Citlali, she'd do it herself. I was furious about having to keep her secrets again. I knew Citlali would never forgive me if she found out; she'd be devastated.

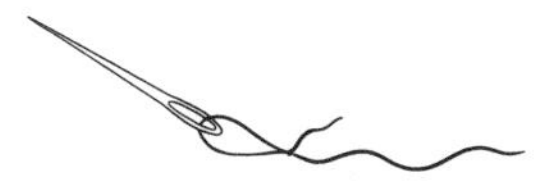

Among the pre-Hispanic Maya, the deity of the moon and weaving sometimes goes by the name of Ixchel, sometimes Ix Chebel Yax. She appears as a very young woman (waxing moon) or very old (waning moon), at times with a coiled serpent headdress and lizard's claws. She is also the goddess of pregnancy, childbirth, medicine, painting, the waters, and the rainbow. And sometimes she sends floods. She is known as Lady of the Rainbow, Only Lady of Cloth, or First Lady of the Brush because she painted the world of colors and also invented hieroglyphic writing. In addition, she is at times called Ix Sacal Uoh—Spider-Weaver—which can also be Ix Sacal Ooh: Interweaver of Glyphs.

In the Maya spoken in Yucatán, the most common verb used for weaving is *sakal*, which is related to the name of the goddess. In the Ch'olan language, the verb for weave is *hal*, a homophone of the word meaning to speak, and which can also mean truth.

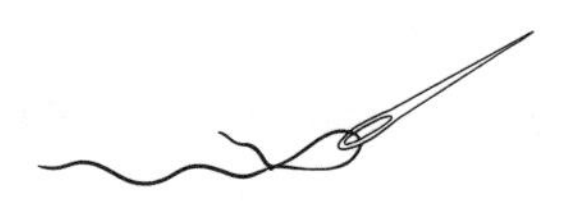

Donna Haraway refigures cat's cradle games, Navajo textiles, the crochet coral reef made by the Wertheim sisters, and other forms of weaving to talk about the possible relationships of responsibility and care between human and non-human creatures. Those, among other projects and practices, seem to her essential for considering and creating more visible political ecologies: for reconstructing the present.

No one had said it straight out, but all the rituals seemed to suggest that our first day at college marked the end of adolescence and our crash landing in adult life. Our whole adolescence could be seen as a preparation for that day: the accumulation of the theoretical, practical, objective, and subjective knowledge we needed to pass through those doors.

We were aware, of course, that adolescence hadn't at heart been, and still wasn't, any of those things. It was the name adults gave to the period of time our bodies needed to acquire their (more or less) permanent shape and size. And that was what life was all about then: our inept, deformed, changing, painful, stimulating, delicious, awful bodies.

For my first day at college, I wore a black skirt and my favorite red blouse: party clothes. I thought of the equivalent day at middle school, of how uncomfortable and sad I'd felt, and was certain that this one would be the complete opposite: a triumph. It wasn't. I was one of the first to arrive and, from my seat, watched the room fill up with women (the majority, and all very different) and a few men. Based on appearance, I attempted to decide which of those women might become my friends, but it was hard to say. The welcoming session was led by a short professor with long bangs and wearing suspenders, who warned us from the outset, and in no uncertain terms, that we weren't going to become writers. We were going to learn to be readers, were going to read the works of hundreds of authors who had written, were writing, and would always write better than we did, with their robust cultural knowledge, their extensive vocabulary, their ability to express their wisdom and revelations in metaphor, ellipsis, synecdoche, and other mysterious terms. It would be best for us to understand once and for all that, after those authors, writing would be mere insolence, a waste of effort.

It hadn't been clear to me that I actually wanted to be a writer until I was told that I wasn't going to be one. I complained to Dalia on behalf of those whose hope it was to write, pretending that I wasn't one of them, but I guess she suspected I was faking. It made no difference to her because her sole interest was in reading and learning about language, history, and literature. I found that attitude inconceivable, like someone loving pools but having absolutely no interest in swimming, like someone studying the history of gastronomy but hating to cook. I didn't believe her, thought it was false modesty, timidity, or, as in my case, lack of confidence. Humility never occurred to me; that Dalia perhaps lacked the necessary level of vanity and ambition if not to write, then to publish.

At least it was clear that we were going to read. I read all the time: in the library, in parks, in bed, and it was delicious to spend days as if underwater, diving from book to book, submerged among literary shipwrecks, mountains, and reefs. Some of the female lecturers and one or two of the men managed to infect us with their enthusiasms, their attention to language, theory, and history. That was enough.

Despite the words of the suspendered professor, I continued to write. In boring classes, during our free time, or at night, I wrote. I invented stories about vampires and frogwomen. And in a blue notebook, I worked slowly on a novel about the friendship between a fugitive and a witch who couldn't speak. Without telling anyone, I wrote in smaller and smaller notebooks, in an awful, almost illegible hand. Just once, I copied out a little of my story about the mute witch and sent it to Citlali.

There's an extremely long piece of work by the Colombian artist María Angélica Medina that she knitted during her exhibitions while chatting to any member of the public who came along. The work is called *Conversación*.

The novel never had a title. The protagonist's name was Susana, and her muteness was caused by forgetting; she'd lived alone for so long that she'd lost the ability to speak. Her isolation had turned her into a sort of witch who could read the truth about the world in the materials around her: air, water, plants, and the stars. One day, a stranger who knew how to talk with animals came to her house. She took him in but soon learned that he was pursuing a woman from afar and was planning to seduce Susana and persuade her to help him to capture the fugitive so he could become the Sultan of a distant kingdom. Susana fled in search of the woman, to warn and assist her. The fugitive's name was Maya, and she was walking through the desert, guarded by two tigers. Susana accompanied her in her exile for several days, and as she was unable to communicate with her through speech, she began to draw in the sand with a stick. They gradually came to understand each other through those images and became friends, and Maya taught Susana her language. That's as far as I got. I never knew how the novel ended.

Violeta Parra also sewed *arpilleras*: Chilean communal appliqué storycloths. In the Louvre, she exhibited a huge tapestry named *La Rebelión de los Campesinos*. There's a video in which she talks about some of the characters in the tapestry, saying they "love peace" and that the flowers sprouting from their heads represent their souls. One of the characters is a self-portrait, depicted in violet, like her name.

Years later, during the Pinochet dictatorship, a group of women known as *las arpilleras* emerged who embroidered narrative tapestries telling the stories of their disappeareds, denouncing the violence of the regime, and demanding justice. Their works were smuggled out of the country to inform the world of the atrocities being perpetrated by the dictatorship. When the authorities learned of this, *las arpilleras* were declared enemies of state and were hounded relentlessly.

On the right side of her black mane (all trace of the red streak she'd once sported has vanished), Dalia has a new shock of pure white hair. Her mother had gone prematurely gray too. It's the first thing I notice when we embrace at the door. She's wearing a red coat and seems a little taller than before; I know she can't have grown, so perhaps it's me who's shrunk—breastfeeding had caused a slight curvature of my spine. We hold each other tightly—with equal force, it seems to me—for a few moments. Without letting go, I say how happy I am to see her, that I've missed her so much. Me too, she replies, and kisses my cheek.

She sits down, I pour her a glass of water, and we talk about her trip. Her accent has changed very little, but now she interjects *a ver* and *vamos* all the time. She brings me up to date on her life: These days she's living with her nonbinary partner. Things had ended badly with the Puerto Rican woman, just a short while before she started dating them. We've been living together for a couple of months in Gracia, she tells me; they work nearby. I've never had to switch pronouns like this before and feel intimidated, so I try to copy her, and speak slowly, afraid of messing up. Dalia, on the other hand, does it fluidly, naturally, as if she'd always used the third-person plural in this way. Suddenly, I'm having difficulty remembering how she used to speak.

She sits on the loveseat, and I join her there. After we've more or less caught up with our lives and I've showed her a video of my daughter—she'd started nursery school a day or two before (it wasn't so bad, I only cried a little)— playing the maracas and dancing to a Pedro Infante song, the silence begins to feel dense, as if filled with Citlali. Neither of us has the courage to broach the subject until I make up my mind to start at one corner—the way you do a jigsaw puzzle. Have you spoken to Valentina again? I ask. I went by to see her yesterday. So how did it go? She tells me that the urn has arrived, that it is in that moron's house. I tell her that I've been to see the ashes and it was horrendous; I wanted to steal them. Dalia sits looking at me without saying a word, and I end up having to break the silence again. I know we're not exactly sure what he did to her and maybe I'm just being totally paranoid, but he didn't give her the love she needed, and for that, if nothing else, I hate him. In part I'm saying this to get in ahead of any reproaches from Dalia, but she tells me she knows a little more now. Valentina told her that Gilberto abused Citlali's mother before her death. He didn't hit her or anything, but when she was pregnant he once or twice threatened to kill her if she divorced him. I feel a cold sweat at the back of my neck, and I tell Dalia that he most likely said things like that to Citlali too. I say that my inability to help her has left me feeling impotent. There was no way we could have, responds Dalia; we loved her as best we could and that's that. All we can do now is to keep on fighting for other women.

But shouldn't we try to do something? He's dangerous. But we have no proof, Dalia replies, and then immediately changes the subject: The good news is that those aren't Citlali's ashes.

I don't understand, so Dalia explains: Valentina—whom it seems Citlali confided in, a fact that makes me ridiculously jealous—told her that on her last night in Senegal, she'd taken Citlali's urn (it was in her room) and emptied it into the sea. Although the night was very dark and she couldn't see well, she waited until she felt sure they'd sunk or floated away. She said her farewells, cried, and then filled the urn with sand.

So how did the sand get through the customs checks at the airport? I ask. No idea, said Dalia. Well, that's a relief, I respond, but there's no note of relief in my voice. I don't want to cry alone, to start crying and not have Dalia crying with me. If I can manage to say nothing for a while, the feeling will surely pass, but I'm unable to hold out and a childish sob emerges as I say, What happened to her? I don't understand the first thing.

Dalia's eyes are sad, but still she doesn't cry. She lowers her head and tells me what Valentina said. Citlali had been depressed and undernourished for quite a long time. Other members of the organization had told her that a few days before her death, a psychiatrist prescribed her strong antidepressants that left her drowsy and numbed. The body needs time to adapt to them. That morning, before going for a swim, Citlali had taken her pills. And that's why she didn't put up a struggle when she was caught in the current.

And she knew. She went into the sea knowing how dangerous it was. I can't stop asking myself what I could have done differently to save her. I feel I failed her, never knew how to help. It wasn't possible, says Dalia. She was so deeply wounded, like a jug full of holes. When we managed to plug one, the water poured out from another. But if it's any help, I *do* believe it was an accident.

I wasn't so sure. That day at Notre Dame, I say, I thought she wanted to jump. Dalia grasped my arm: That's exactly why I say it was an accident—she didn't want to die in the sea.

But she did want to die, didn't she? It might have been an accident, but she still wanted to die. Dalia nods, says she thinks a part of her *did* want to die.

The pauses between our comments grow longer.

If she intended it, says Dalia, it was like a gift to us to arrange it this way, to allow us to think it was an accident.

And if someone dies accidentally, but wanted to die, is that still suicide? I ask.

Scanning my bookshelves, Dalia says dying like that is good luck, a way for Citlali to finally rest.

To finally rest, I echo, trying to feel convinced.

I'm not so certain. What if she didn't want to die? I ask. If that's true, her death was very unfair. Whatever the case, it's wrong, it's unfair and sad, says Dalia, and she puts her arms around me again. Her hair smells of a mildly citric-scented shampoo, and I sense that she's crying too, that slow tears are dampening her sweater.

As I move away to find a tissue, I hear her say, It's a good death, drowning in the sea, leaving your ashes in the sea. Citlali said something like that once, after I gave her those books on Buddhism. Remember? She said we're like waves in the sea, an illusion of the tides.

Yes, she said something like that to me too. And she liked stories about pirates and seafarers, I add, wiping away my remaining tears. She loved that Nick Cave song about the ship.

I tell Dalia about the reading list in her bedroom. She smiles.

Are you going to the leave-taking? I ask. Ugh, don't know. I don't want to see Gilberto. Me neither, I respond, but I'm organizing it, so I guess I have to be there. Come with me. Dalia promises she will.

We go on talking about Citlali for a long time, say her name over and again, like a spell to conjure her up. I think we almost manage it.

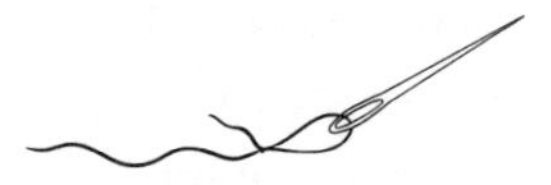

I repeat these words by Ovid like a mantra: "Grief brings great inspiration and ingenuity outwits disaster."

Louise Bourgeois decided to become an assassin of her work to avoid being one in real life. In an interview she says, “To be an artist is a guarantee to your fellow humans that the wear and tear of living will not let you become a murderer.” Using a needle and thread, she wounds but also heals the bodies of her sculptures. She is part surgeon, part seamstress, part artist. In the conjunction of these three activities, in the needle and thread, there must be some answer.

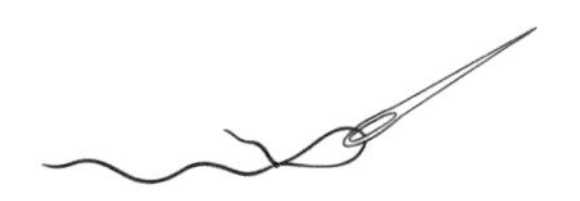

There are ten of us in the Viveros de Coyoacán. Guillermo arrived with Valentina and the other aunts. Dalia and I are sitting on a pair of tree stumps, and the others are on the ground, under the cypresses we liked so much when we were in middle school. We’re all holding brown paper bags filled with peanuts in their shells.

Apparently feeding the squirrels is prohibited, I

say to Dalia, pointing to a rusty sign. Why? she asks. It must be because they're bad for them, or because squirrels are pests. I respond.

The squirrels are less shy now; there are two close to me, one gray and one black. I shoo them away with my hand, and my daughter happily chases them.

I don't think of them as cute, says Dalia; they're ugly animals. A bit neurotic, I reply, but who isn't? The two squirrels return, accompanied by another, dark brown one. I guess we should ask if anyone wants to say a few words, I whisper. In a while, Dalia replies. Let's just sit in silence a little longer.

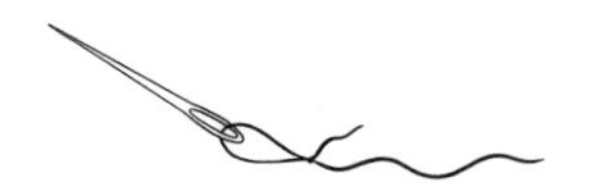

The greater part of Cecilia Vicuña's work involves weaving, braiding, intertwining threads and words on paper, fabric, and in the voice. I'm borrowing these lines from her:

> The weaver sees her fiber as the poet sees her word.
>
> The thread feels the hand, as the word feels the tongue…
>
> A word is pregnant with other words and a thread contains other threads within its interior.

To speak is to thread and the thread weaves the world…

The word and the thread behave in the same way as processes of the cosmos.

Citlali was sitting barefoot and cross-legged on the couch in pajamas, embroidering a design of yellow fish on a black background. They're deep-sea fish, she tells me, and reels off a list of the scientific names. It was eight in the morning. Citlali guessed that Dalia had returned during the night and then gone out again very early. She hadn't seen her, but had heard the door open and close. I went to the kitchen, nibbled a little fruit, and, when I returned, found Citlali holding my black embroidery. Her eyes were closed, and she was slowly stroking the threads with a fingertip. I didn't want to interrupt her, so I stood there, watching how she read the braille of the embroidery. When she opened her eyes, she said she liked the idea of reducing the work to texture and touch, of embroidering for the skin so it could be sensed in the dark. She made some good suggestions for one part of the design where I was still unsure of which stitches to use.

We sat a while in silence, hoping for Dalia to return, then Citlali said she knew about Dalia and Scorpion. Dalia had written to tell her, and if it had been any other time she'd have been completely *tusa. Tusa*? I interrupted. That's what they say in Colombia when you're heartbroken. She rephrased: At any other time she'd have been furious or terribly upset, or both, but she'd read the message that day when she'd had no money for food, and the whole business of Dalia and Scorpion had seemed remote, unimportant. That day, she said, she'd remembered how it felt to be hungry. Most of the time, it wasn't something she experienced, but on that day she'd felt hungry for the first time in ages, and that overshadowed Dalia's news, made it insignificant. Hunger was what mattered. I said I was glad—not that she'd been hungry, but that she realized that the Dalia-Scorpion thing was no big deal. I begged her never to get into that state again, never to go without food. I said it was lucky her aunt had wired money, but if she didn't find work, she'd have to return to Mexico. Period. She neither agreed nor disagreed. I tried to recall that poem by Auden called "First Things First," about how essentials like drinking water must always take precedence over love, but only scattered phrases came to my mind.

A short while later Dalia returned, looking pleased with herself; she'd summoned up the courage to go out alone and hadn't gotten lost. Plus she'd understood a lot more French than she'd thought. The night before, she'd gone to an event at the Louvre, with chamber orchestras playing in different rooms and actors reciting poetry to the music. That morning, she'd visited the catacombs; she had taken photos of the skulls and promised to show them to us later.

It was our last full day in Paris, and we strolled along the narrow streets of the Latin Quarter to the Musée de Cluny: the three of us walking together. We saw various busts of bearded men, a golden flower, and illuminated manuscripts. Citlali translated from French the parts of the labels we didn't understand. Dalia translated the Latin inscriptions we didn't understand; I told them the story of the narwhal horns, the many theories of the invention of unicorns.

We reached the huge tapestries of The Lady and the Unicorn and sat down to contemplate them. The wall text said they were thought to have been woven by more than one generation of women: whole lives of female friends, mothers, and daughters entwined in the threads, in the flora and fauna on the same enormous cloth. Five of the tapestries represented the senses, and the sixth, of the lady, was free will.

Just outside the museum we found a crepe cart. We were hoping that Dalia would have the courage to ask for hers in French, but she didn't. Citlali did the ordering, and we wolfed down our food.

We were walking along Boulevard Saint-Michel when a tall man with a shaved head and a beard spoke to me. I was wearing a rounded red cap with fake fur lining, like Eskimo headgear, and the man asked if I was from Mongolia. His mistake must have been due to the shape of my eyes and my black hair, and the idea of resembling a Mongolian woman pleased me. I told him I was from Mexico and walked quickly on, but he sped up too and wanted to know if the others were my sisters. I said they were to avoid any more questions and moved on. We came to a bookstore, and I suggested to Dalia and Citlali that we go in to shake the man off. It worked. I took advantage of our diversion to buy a French copy of *The Three Musketeers*, which had been my favorite novel as a child. I didn't care that my French might not be good enough to read the book; I was sure I'd manage it sooner or later.

It was dark by the time we left the bookstore, and we had a long journey home on the metro. On the train, we found four seats together and Citlali and I sat down on one side, with Dalia facing us, with an empty space beside her. When we had just a few stations to go, Dalia took out her embroidery bag, as she wanted to correct something, perhaps unpick a stitch that had turned out badly. Her eyes were fixed on the fabric, but at some point she lifted them, and something behind Citlali and me, in the center of the car, caught her attention. She grabbed Citlali's knee, leaned across to us, and whispered, Don't turn around, but we need to get off at the next stop. I'll explain when we're on the platform. Citlali obeyed; I immediately turned my head. The man who had approached me in the boulevard was strap-hanging a few yards from us and was exposing himself: His penis was thick, erect, purple, veiny, and had a piercing running through it with a round stud on either end. His face was expressionless, except perhaps for his eyes, which were fixed on us. No one else in the car seemed to have noticed him. Nobody said anything. He stood there like an apparition, like something from a nightmare. I turned back and saw that Dalia was firmly gripping her poultry scissors in one hand. Underneath was her embroidery—scarlet flowers surrounded by dark leaves, like ivy. The sleeve of her coat had rolled back a little, and I thought I glimpsed one of those pale scars on her forearm. A barrage of questions assaulted me, filling the moment of tension: How had she made those cuts? With a knife? What knife? The X-Acto knife we'd used in our technical drawing class? With scissors? With those poultry scissors? I could feel the blood pulsing in the veins of my neck and squeezed Citlali's hand tight. She stared at Dalia in concern, but with complete faith in her judgment. I didn't know what was going on with the man, but Dalia kept holding her scissors and I automatically extracted a needle from the red needle wallet peeking out of her bag. Visions passed before my eyes of the possible attack. I imagined the man coming up to us and Dalia snipping off his penis. The penis falling to the ground and rolling away, leaving a trail of blood on the floor of the train. I decided I'd have to steel myself to stick the needle in his eye.

None of that happened. At the next station, we

jumped off the train and ran until the doors closed again. Then, without slowing down, we turned to check that the man wasn't behind us, hadn't gotten off at the same stop. When we saw that the platform was empty, we stopped, and that's when I realized that I was still holding the needle. I'd gripped it so tightly that it had dug into my palm, and a trickle of blood was running down my wrist and into the sleeve of my coat. I pulled the needle out and raised my palm to my mouth to suck the blood, then hid my hand in my pocket. I put my free arm around Citlali's shoulders, and Dalia took her hand, repeating in a firm tone, It's over. In her right hand, Dalia was still holding the scissors. We walked more slowly for a while, getting our breath back. Citlali asked what had happened, what was happening, and Dalia gave her the gist of the story, that there had been a man on the train exposing himself. She didn't mention that it was the same person who'd approached us earlier, that his penis was erect, and that he was staring straight at us. Nor did she mention the piercing, so Citlali wouldn't be able to imagine it. Very soon we were laughing, sometimes quietly in relief, sometimes loaded with fear, with tears not far away.

On our way back to the apartment, we walked the dark streets, our arms intertwined like threads in the fabric of time. Still a little nervous, but also excited and feeling the cold, we stopped at the window of a toy store, only dimly lit by a patch of light from a streetlamp.

In the shadows, we could see puppets, wooden dolls, and charmless rag clowns. We spent some time gazing into the dark toy store, which was like something from a dream, a shadowy dream from our childhood. As though the three of us were dreaming the same dream on that last night of our trip.

Citlali had to leave for the train station before we set off for the airport. We hugged her goodbye at the door of the building—she allowed me to hug her tightly—wished her bon voyage, and asked her to let us know when she arrived in Provence. Our return flight was silent and slightly nostalgic, as return flights generally are; we slept almost the whole time.

Classes restarted. Our schedules didn't coincide much that semester, but on Tuesdays I had the same lunch hour as Dalia, so we usually ate together. We were still close, although in hindsight I can see how we'd started to move apart, the way the strands of an old piece of thread eventually uncoil.

A few months later, I received a letter in the mail from Citlali. Inside the envelope were a postcard and a single sheet of paper, the words written in black ink. The postcard was of a world map, across which she'd embroidered a dotted red line with a small boat floating on it. She'd also sewn a circle on France, another on Mexico, a question mark on Colombia, and another on

Brazil. On the back, she complained about the Mexican postal system, said that as her message would probably not arrive until after she was supposed to have returned to Mexico, I'd have realized she wasn't coming back. By the time I read her postcard, she'd either be with her friend Yanina in Colombia or doing that voluntary work in Brazil—she still hadn't made up her mind. She talked about how much she'd enjoyed our trip to Paris and about the hundreds of trips we still had to make before she boarded her boat to sail through the last years of her life.

I search "Senegal beaches" and "Senegal drowning" on the internet and imagine it, or rather decide to imagine it, like this:

She woke early, which was unusual because she'd been sleeping for almost ten hours lately. She ate a slice of toast and an apple, then swallowed the pill the doctor had prescribed. It was her free day; some of her colleagues had planned a trip to the island of Gorée, but she felt like swimming alone off the beach.

After a few earlier failed attempts, she'd figured out

the best way to get there and waited on the corner for the brightly colored bus to arrive. She sat in the back and, looking out the window as the bus rattled along, saw a cart being pulled by a horse, a small sidewalk market, an ox, and several half-built breezeblock houses. When they were approaching her stop, she rapped loudly on the window. She walked past restaurants, multicolored boats, and children with radiant smiles playing football. When she came to the shore, a man offered to take her to Ngor Island in a piragua. Ten minutes later she was on her favorite beach. She chose a restaurant at random, ordered eggs and mineral water, and, adding a tip, asked the waiter to keep an eye on her backpack while she went for a swim before her meal arrived. She walked quite a long way, until she came to the surfer beach, then picked her way through the black rocks on the shoreline and swam out, breaking up the patterns of the surf with her strokes, diving under when a big wave came along. There were very few surfers around that day. She swam on to the tune of a song from childhood that suddenly came into her head: "To the sea I came for oranges, but oranges are not found in the sea." Still singing, she imagined rising sea levels causing the beach and then the whole island to disappear. She tried to sense the increased acidity of the water on her skin. And then the song made her think that she needed to buy fruit, and also reminded her of a story her grandmother had given her like a gift not long before her death—the story of an old woman and her dog who were waiting on a surfboard for a large wave. The old woman went back and forth from the beach, bringing along more and more accessories each time until the board ended up looking like a circus, but even so she managed to ride the wave and rescue a little girl who was drowning.

At that point, she realized she was a long way from the shore and began to swim back, but the current was very strong, stronger than any she'd swum in before, and she was alarmed to find that however hard she tried, she was being carried farther out to sea. Her arms were tiring. She saw some fishermen in the distance and attempted to attract their attention. Thinking they had perhaps seen her, she waited. She wasn't frightened. A combination of fatigue and the medication was making her increasingly sleepy—she was withdrawing, switching off, and then began to lose consciousness. Finally, a wave swept over her like a freshly laundered sheet embroidered with spume.

I tell myself that if she fell asleep and never woke, in some way she is still dreaming now.

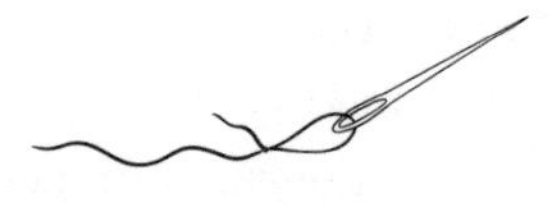

I've searched for us in many books and found scraps of us in some, maybe particularly in Fleur Jaeggy's *Sweet*

Days of Discipline. There's a passage that speaks of a "double image" that is "anatomical and antique. In the one the girl runs about and laughs, and in the other she lies on a bed covered by a lace shroud. It's her own skin has embroidered it."

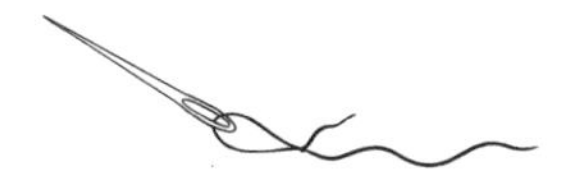

After a while, Dalia reads the messages Citlali's friends have sent from other countries. Valentina plays the guitar and sings a sweet, sad song about dying so as to fly away. When she's finished, I ask Dalia if she'd like to say a few words, but she shakes her head. I read Christina Rossetti's poem "Song," which I've spent a long time trying to translate into Spanish. Even the first lines—"When I am dead, my dearest / Sing no sad songs for me."—were hard because in Spanish *dearest* has to be gendered. Should it be *queridísima* or *queridísimo*? I finally opted for the feminine form. After a few more speeches and some amusing or heartwarming stories about Citlali, Gilberto invites us all home. I'm not interested, but I turn to Dalia and she says yes, so we both go.

We enter the apartment together. On the table are trays of canapés, which excite my daughter. The other guests sit down, but Dalia and I remain on our feet, near Citlali's ashes. Gilberto comes over, carrying a glass of wine. Here's to my daughter! he says. *Salud*, we respond unwillingly, and he moves on to talk to other people. The canapés are quite good, I tell Dalia. Not bad at all. At that moment we notice Gilberto stand up unsteadily and head for the bathroom. I wait a moment or two and then offer one hand to Dalia and the other to my daughter and I lead them to Citlali's bedroom. I don't have to tell Dalia what I want to do. My daughter looks curiously at me. I place the embroidery folder in Dalia's hands, take the reading list and the books in their clear plastic wrappers, and we quickly head for the door. We already have it open when Gilberto catches up with us. "Where do you think you're going with all that? They're mementos of my daughter, give them back right now!"

Dalia turns to face him and puts a hand behind her back to signal me to continue on. We were there when she made these things, she yells; the three of us embroidered together thousands of times. We have far more right to them than you.

A slurred expression appears on Gilberto's face, a drunken mix of doubt and disgust, and he gives a very slight nod. Before he can say anything else, Dalia pulls the door shut. Gilberto doesn't try to follow us.

Back at my place, we divvy up the books and tear the reading list in two. We agree to swap when we've read everything on our halves. Then we open the folder. We take out the colored threads and several pieces of fabric with unfinished embroideries. She was still working on this one, I say, passing Dalia the arachniary. It's a piece of cotton fabric covered in hundreds of spiders: daddy long-legs, black widows, wolf and crab spiders, and many more. It's the same piece of cloth she'd worked on in high school, but at some later date she'd embroidered over the original figures. They are now all linked by the threads of different webs, some shaped like leaves, some like funnels or clouds: the last thread always beginning the next piece of embroidery. It's a beautiful, slightly gloomy web. We have to keep working on it, I tell Dalia. There are over 40,000 species of spider, she replies, but we can take it in turns.

Acknowledgements

This novel owes its existence to the generous and close readings of Christina, Chantal, César, Nayeli, Elvira, Marina, Abril, Renata, Astrid, Ana Paula, Sol, and Verónica. Thank you all for your affection and for helping this book to achieve its best possible version. I would also like to offer my thanks to Guillermo, Dulce, Rodrigo, Alejandro, Gustavo, Paty, Vania, Ana Paula, Arianna, Ariana, and the whole team at the wonderful publishing house Almadía, plus everyone at Two Lines Press for making this translation possible. Infinite thanks to Christina for the magic and hard work she brings to this translation. My thanks also go to Andrea and Margarita for their books on Mexican arts; to Rachel, our artistic director; to Antonia for the embroidery classes; to Paula and Andrea for being such a great team; to my mother; Marisa, Margarita, Adolphe, Héctor, and Toumani for sharing childcare and so allowing me time to write this book; to Silvestre, for his endless enthusiasm. And of course, as ever, huge thanks to Alejandro.

In addition to the books mentioned in the text, for the fragments related to embroidery I found the following titles particularly useful: *Textiles de Chiapas* (Artes de México, no. 19), *Textiles de Oaxaca* (Artes de México, no. 35), *Tesoros del arte popular mexicano, colección Nelson A. Rockefeller* (Artes de México), *Embroidery from India and Pakistan* (Sheila Paine, The British Museum), *Embroidery from Afghanistan* (Sheila Paine, The British Museum), *México Bordado, de la tradición al punto contemporáneo* (Gimena Romero, Editorial Gustavo Gili), *The Maya Textile Tradition* (Jeffrey Jay Foxx *et al*, Harry N. Abrams), *Threads of Life* (Clare Hunter, Abrams Press), and *Saberes Enlazados, la obra de Irmgard Weitlaner Johnson* (Kirsten Johnson, Artes de México).

Biographies

JAZMINA BARRERA's books have been published in nine countries and translated to English, Dutch, Italian, and French. Two Lines Press has published two previous books by her, both translated by Christina MacSweeney: *Linea Nigra*, which was a finalist for the National Book Critics Circle Prize in Autobiography and the Greg Barrois Book in Translation Prize; and *On Lighthouses*, which was a finalist for the von Rezzori award and chosen for the Indie Next list by Indie Bound. *Linea Nigra* was also a finalist for CANIEM's Book of the year award and the Amazon Primera Novela (First Novel) Award. She is editor and co-founder of Ediciones Antílope and lives in Mexico City.

CHRISTINA MACSWEENEY's translation of Valeria Luiselli's *The Story of My Teeth* received the Valle Inclán Translation Prize and was also shortlisted for the Dublin Literary Award. In addition to Jazmina Barrera's works, she has published two books by Elvira Navarro for Two Lines Press, including *Rabbit Island*, which was longlisted for a National Book Award. Among her other recent translations are fiction and nonfiction works by Daniel Saldaña París, Verónica Gerber Bicecci, Julián Herbert, and Karla Suárez.

By the Same Author & Translator from Two Lines Press

On Lighthouses

Linea Nigra